PROTECTOR

Ashlee Price

TABLE OF CONTENTS

PROLOGUE

Xander

"Silent night, holy night..."

"Dashing through the snow in a one-horse open sleigh..."

"Fa la la la la la la la la!"

The familiar lyrics of holiday tunes merge into a medley with no rhyme or rhythm above the roar of my motorcycle engine. The strings of colorful lights on the windows blur into a seamless spectrum.

I tighten my grip on the throttle, urging my vehicle to go even faster. The icy, sobering wind sweeps my hair back and numbs my hollowed cheeks.

Damn Tracy for hiding my helmet. As if it wasn't bad enough that she turned off my phone.

The rotten smell of burnt turkey drifting out of an apartment window puts a grimace on my face. Moments later, the aroma of cranberries and perfectly cooked turkey makes my mouth water.

If Tracy had only cooked good turkey like she promised she would, instead of making that excuse for a meatloaf, I would have drunk less. As it was, I had to open a second bottle of wine to cleanse my palate of the rubbery aftertaste.

It was probably part of her strategy to get her hands inside my pants faster. Not that I minded that, though now is neither the time nor the place for reminiscing about that particular episode.

The clamor of church bells, ominous to my ears instead of jubilant, reminds me of the gravity of my current situation. A family is going inside as I drive past the church, and I catch a glimpse of the nativity set on the altar through the open door. For the first time in a long time, I utter a prayer.

Please let me make it in time.

The city's fifty-foot Douglas fir looms over the horizon, then towers over me in all its dazzling glory as I drive around it.

It's an enchanting sight, a reminder of all the warmth and magic the holidays bring.

Unfortunately, tragedies don't take holidays. Even tonight, on Christmas Eve, hell is threatening to break loose.

I only hope that I can shut it down before innocent lives are lost.

Please, please...

The plea gets derailed from the tracks of my thoughts as I hear the wail of the sirens riding on the breeze. My eyes grow wide as I see a curl of smoke blotting out a portion of the night sky. The stench of smoke reaches my nostrils and my jaw clenches.

No.

As the burning building appears before my eyes, the fire worse than I expected, my heart begins to hammer. I crouch on my motorcycle, practically hugging the vehicle as I go even faster, as fast as it allows me to go. The engine roars in protest. The wind stings.

The tires screech against the pavement as I finally stop in between the crimson fire trucks. I let the bike fall as I get off and march to the nearest truck.

"Xander?"

Chester peers at me through narrowed eyes as he speaks between ragged breaths. His charred suit tells me he's just come out of hell. His slumped shoulders are the sign of defeat.

I frown.

"What are you doing here?" he asks.

"Captain said all units," I briefly explain as I grab a set of gear. "Are Martin and Jessie inside?"

"Yeah." Chester nods. "I was just there, too."

But as usual, you chickened out. Coward.

"Xander, you should know..."

"Bolt." Capt. Rick Morrison appears from behind the truck. "What are you doing?"

I zip my suit up. "Getting ready to go in, sir, like you asked."

"I asked you that more than an hour ago," he tells me with a disapproving frown and both hands on his hips. "I didn't hear from you. I assumed you were too busy making out under the mistletoe to help out."

I swallow the bitter lump in my throat. "I'm here now, sir."

"I've already told the team to get out. The building won't hold much longer."

I lift my head to give him a puzzled look. "But there are still dozens of people left in that building. We can't just abandon them."

He shakes his head. "It's too late to save them."

No.

I slip on my boots, grab my helmet and run towards the building.

"Bolt!" The captain calls after me. "Don't go in there! Do you hear me? That's an order."

Fuck it.

"Are you crazy?" Chester shouts behind me. "Don't try to be a hero, man."

No. He's got it wrong. I'm not trying to be a hero. I never have. The only one I'm trying to save is myself.

"Xan—"

4

The explosion in front of me drowns out Chester's voice and every other sound. The thunder buzzes in my ears. The force of it pushes me back and I end up on the pavement. My helmet flies from my hand.

For a moment, I can't move. When I finally try to get up, I notice the pain over my eye. I touch my forehead and feel something damp.

Blood.

A flaming felt Santa ornament a few inches away from me draws my attention. Around me, more burning debris rain down from above.

I grab it and put out the flames with my own hands before clutching it to my chest. As I turn my head towards the fresh pile of charred rubble, my heart stops.

My ears clear just in time for me to hear the echoes of my own scream.

Chapter One

Robyn

Faster!

The command from my brain sends my heart pounding like a war drum. Adrenaline pumps through my veins and my legs spur forward. Long blades of grass tickle my knees.

Faster!

Through a gap between the branches, I catch a glimpse of the sun barely staying afloat in a sea of clouds. None of the weak sunlight filters through the trees to splotch the ground beneath my feet, and no heat scorches my bare skin.

Good. With no sunbeams bouncing off my copper locks, it should be easier to blend in with the trees and the bushes.

A breeze sends the leaves shuddering and sweeps my hair across my face. The thin tendrils stick to my cheeks. Instead of brushing them off, I wear them like a gossamer veil as I continue running.

A stronger breeze blows against my back and an involuntary shiver crawls up my spine. I wrap my arms around my breasts in an effort to ward off the cold.

Clothes would have been nice, but of course, Howie didn't think so. That just goes to show how fucked up he is.

Now I know how the people in that reality show on Discovery Channel feel—naked and afraid. I used to think they were crazy. Now, I feel nothing but admiration for them.

It takes guts to survive.

And I have that, at least.

Guts, yes. Stamina, no.

My chest starts to hurt as my lungs fall behind. In spite of the cool air, a sheen of sweat moistens my forehead and my throat dries up. A burning sensation starts to grip my sides and the backs of my legs. My feet grow heavier by the second.

This is what I get for not going to the gym as often as I should, even though we have one on the fifth floor.

Still, I keep running.

My life depends on it. If I stop, Howie or one of his men will catch up to me, and I'd rather die than go back to being his plaything.

The mere memory of his fingertips grazing my skin makes me cringe. My resolve turns to steel and gives me a new pair of lungs and legs.

Faster!

A low branch cuts across my cheek, narrowly missing my eye. I trip over a rock and end up rolling down a slope. My skin gets scraped in a dozen different places and covered in dirt everywhere else.

Still, I run. My chest heaves as I gasp for air and I open my mouth to let more in. A bead of sweat rolls down the side of my face.

I stop only after I stumble again. This time, I fall forward on my arms and my palm lands smack on top of the sharp tip of a broken branch. I open my mouth in a silent scream at the pain before lifting my hand and turning it around. My blood paints the lines red.

Shit.

I see a fragment of wood in the slit where the blood is trickling out. I draw a deep breath, grit my teeth, and pull it out. After I toss it aside I clasp my hands together to try to stop the bleeding, and when that fails I clench my fist around a lock of my hair instead. It's the next best thing I have to fabric.

Now my hair is really red.

A sound reaches my ears and I turn my head. I recognize it as the whir of an automobile engine. My chest swells with relief.

Cars—which means there's a road just up ahead, which in turn means I might just be able to escape.

Freedom at last.

Brimming with hope, I lift my foot to put it forward and continue running, but another sound, this time that of heavy footsteps approaching, glues me where I stand. A twig snaps beneath a boot a few feet behind me and my heart stops.

They're here.

"Here, kitty, kitty, kitty," one of them starts calling.

Vaughn.

I don't know what his first name is. Howie always calls him Vaughn. For all I know, that could be his first name.

It doesn't matter. All I know is that he's dangerous. He said it himself while whittling a piece of pine wood with a pocket knife that gleamed as brightly as his sinister grin.

Trust Howie to find men as sick as he is.

Careful not to make a sound, I quickly scoot behind a tree.

"Her name is Robyn, you ass," another man speaks.

He's smarter than Vaughn but not nearly half as big, a fact that he's tried to conceal by covering nearly every inch of his body in swirling tattoos. I know because he asked me to soap him once. With Howie's permission.

"Shut up, minifucker!" That's Vaughn's pet name for Tom. "Who said I was talking to you?"

"What did you call me again?"

Vaughn replies with a deep laugh that rumbles through the woods.

"Why, you..."

They're fighting again.

Good. As long as they're not working together or focusing on finding me, I have a chance of escaping.

I stare straight ahead, trying to locate the road. Just then I hear another car passing by, and I seize my chance.

I crawl across the ground as quietly as I can until I no longer hear them bickering like high school girls in the locker hall. Then I hide behind another tree and turn my head to look over my shoulder.

I can still see their bulky outlines in the distance.

It's a good distance, though.

Another car passes by, the hum of the engine louder this time.

Almost there.

I draw a deep breath and sprint in the direction of the road without a backward glance.

This is it. It's all or nothing.

Please don't let them see me. Please...

"There she is!"

Shit.

I ignore the sound of approaching footsteps and run faster than I ever have in my entire life.

"Robyn!"

"Stop, bitch! You have nowhere to go!"

Maybe he's right. It's been a while since I've had anyplace I really belong. Still, anywhere is better than back in Howie's house, however grand it is.

Finally, I break out of the woods and reach the road. The warm, coarse asphalt is a welcome change beneath my feet, but the moment I step on it, blots of rain begin to fall.

I keep running. Through the cascade of raindrops bombarding the pavement and hitting my skin like bullets, my eyes scan my surroundings in a desperate search for a way out of my predicament.

Please...

Relief washes over me as I see a truck parked along the side of the road past the curve, its back open.

An answered prayer.

I glance over my shoulder just once to make sure neither Tom nor Vaughn has caught up to me yet. When I don't see their shadows, I run towards the truck and climb inside.

Piles of boxes stand against all sides of the compartment. I hide behind one of them as I hear someone approaching.

A moment later, the metal doors close with a bang. For the first time in days, the sound is not one of doom but salvation. I also hear something else, most likely a padlock sliding into place, as a man mumbles, "That's better."

A few moments more and the truck starts moving again. I let out the breath I've been holding for the longest time as a sigh of relief while I rest my head against the side of a box. I hug my tired knees to my still heaving chest and a drop of rain that has become ensnared in my hair falls on one of them.

My hair falls like a curtain over my face and knees as I bury my face in my arms. The splatter of the shards of sky against the top and sides of the truck mirrors the pounding of my heart, which eventually slows down as the rain picks up. My breathing grows even, too, as my mind and body slip into a state of ease.

Finally, I'm safe.

I'd jump up and down at the victory, but I'm too tired. I don't even have enough strength in my arm to manage a fist pump. My eyelids fall shut, and in minutes the symphony of the downpour along with the motion of the truck lull me into a much-needed restful sleep.

~

A crash against my eardrums jars my senses and jolts me out of sleep.

At first, I think it's a clap of thunder and the sliver of light at its heels a bolt of lightning. As the sliver broadens, though, and the brightness blinds my eyes, my mind clears. My memories return like scenes falling into place on a reel.

I escaped. I got inside a truck and then I fell asleep.

As I wipe the stain of saliva from the corner of my mouth, I look around at the towers of boxes surrounding me.

I'm still inside the truck. It's stopped now, and the doors are thrown wide open once more, just like when I found it.

As that realization sinks in, panic seizes me.

The truck stopped? Did Howie find me? Have I been caught?

The voices that reach my ears are unfamiliar, though, so my fear is apparently unfounded. A fresh wave of relief washes over me and the knots in my shoulders unravel.

It's fine. I'm fine. I've managed to escape.

The truck has simply stopped because it has reached its destination, wherever that is. I don't care where as long as it's a good many miles away from Howie.

Of course, I still don't know where I'm going or what I'm supposed to do now. Heck, I don't even know where to get clothes.

As I look down at my still naked body, covered in dirt and scrapes of all sizes, another realization dawns on me.

So far, all the voices I've heard have been male. True, they may not belong to Howie or Vaughn or Tom or Jeff, but they belong to grown men just like them, men who could very well act just like them. Well, maybe they won't lock me up and have me walk around on a leash, or ask me to soap them and feed them, but what guarantee do I have that they won't try to grab me? After all, I don't have any clothes on, and some men might take that as a coupon for a free fuck.

I shake my head. No. I didn't escape hell just to end up in another god-forsaken abyss.

I get on my feet, poised to make yet another escape. As soon as I turn around, though, my eyes clash with a pair of ebony ones. They grow wide, then scour me from top to bottom before their owner, a lanky man in his mid-forties wearing a checkered red shirt with its sleeves rolled halfway, steps back.

"Holy shit!"

I, too, stumble back in shock, then quickly fold my legs beneath me as I turn to one side. I cross my arms over my breasts as well and let my hair cascade past my shoulders in a poor attempt to cover myself.

"What's wrong?" another male voice asks.

A moment later, a shadow falls on me. I slowly turn my head, and this time my eyes collide with twin kaleidoscopes of gray, green and gold set amid chiseled features which exude elegance and strength all at once.

I blink and resist the urge to pinch myself.

Am I sure I'm awake? Because this guy looks like a dream.

"Whoa."

His lips—the upper barely visible and the lower thick—form an oval as he brushes the strands of bronze hair up to reveal a broad, scarred forehead.

I slide back while trying to keep myself covered. My shoulder hits a box. I catch a glimpse of a pair of pliers inside it and pull it out.

"Don't come any closer." I brandish the tool like a weapon.

"Easy." He raises his hands. "I'm not going to hurt you."

My eyebrows furrow.

He's not?

I point the pliers straight at him. "Like hell I believe you."

After all I've been through, I don't think I can ever trust a man again.

He grabs the back of his black shirt and pulls it over his neck, then offers it to me.

"Wear this. You must be cold."

I glance at the shirt. My eyebrows grow even more crooked.

He's giving me his shirt?

I direct my gaze back at him and my eyes fall on his ripped torso. Each section is well-defined. His carved pectorals, coated with just a few wisps of hair, bulge out over rows of hard abs. The distinct trail between each half of his belly disappears beneath the waistband of his jeans. Long, toned arms hang from broad shoulders, one extended towards me and the other resting at his side.

My mouth waters and my hand gripping the pliers drops to my side.

I know I haven't been praying. Why then does it seem like I've come face to face with some sort of god?

"Go on," he urges.

I swallow the lump in my throat and put down the pliers so I can grab the shirt. As soon as I do, he turns around.

My wide eyes follow the waves of his hair down to his nape... and further down.

His back does not have as many ridges or bulges as his front, but it still manages to take my breath away. Even with the massive bird—a phoenix?—inked on his back, I can still make out the fit bands of muscle.

Strange. I've seen Vaughn and Tom's bare backs, but I've never been this fascinated. Maybe it's because I knew they were monsters, heartless vermin, worse than animals.

This man may look battle-ready, savage even, with raw masculinity coming off him in waves. But he's neither a monster nor a beast.

He's a man among men, the kind women like me have no chance of resisting.

Already, I can feel a fire kindling inside my chest, the heat spreading all the way up to my neck and filling my cheeks. My breasts tingle. My pulse quickens and excitement flutters through my veins.

My eyes remain glued to him and my fingers long to get lost in his hair and trace the curves of his muscles.

I tear my gaze away from him, though, and shake my head. I pat my cheeks and draw in a deep breath to extinguish the flames beneath my skin.

What am I doing, acting like an animal in heat?

I slip my arms through the sleeves of the shirt, but pause before putting it on as the letters printed on the back catch my attention.

SFPD.

My eyebrows arch. He's a cop?

That explains why I feel like I can trust him and why he's physically fit. Still, I've never seen a cop this hot.

Curious, I lift the black cotton to my nostrils and catch a whiff of detergent beneath the musk of sweat.

Not a bad combination. In fact, I find it strangely nice, addicting even.

I frown. First my eyes. Now my nose.

This man is snatching my senses one by one.

I pull the shirt over my head. The loose fabric slides over my chest and conceals my breasts from view in more ways than one. The sleeves droop and cover my entire upper arms.

Good.

The only problem is that the loose neckline dips a little too low for my liking, but that's fine. After being naked for so long, I'm not complaining.

I stand up, pull my hair out from beneath the shirt so it still flows past my shoulders, and pull the hem as far down as it can go, which is midway past my thigh.

When I lift my head, I find him staring at me and a blush coats my cheeks anew.

Why is he looking at me more intently now that I'm clothed? It almost makes me feel naked again.

18

I cross my arms over my chest and pout.

"What are you looking at?"

"Nothing," he answers. "The shirt looks better on you than it did on me."

My heart stops. Is that a compliment?

Nonsense. There's no way I'd look good in this oversized shirt, not with my hair a mess and my skin still badly in need of washing.

He offers me his hand. "There should be more clothes in my trailer."

I glance at my bare legs.

"And food and water. And coffee. You can take a shower, too."

All those sound good.

But can I really trust this man?

"Don't worry. You're safe now," he says. "No one will hurt you. You have my word."

Maybe it's the conviction in his voice or maybe it's because of that look of genuine concern in his eyes—or maybe it's just his muscles blinding me and making it impossible for me to think straight—but I find myself believing him.

I could use the help. Besides, he's a cop. Maybe I can trust him.

I step forward slowly and his lips curve into a smile which takes my breath away. My fingers dance across his palm and the simple contact messes with my heart again.

And with my coordination.

I stumble over the edge of the truck. With unbelievable reflexes, he catches me and pulls me right into his arms. My breasts press against his bare chest.

I lift my head slowly to look into his eyes. My cheeks burn.

For a moment, I can't speak. Even my lips are under his spell now, and all they want to do is kiss him. I manage to pull away, though. I avert my gaze, gripping the neckline of the shirt with one hand and pulling the hem down with the other as I squeeze my thighs close together.

What in the world is wrong with me?

"My name is Alexander," he introduces as he offers his hand anew while the other strokes the sprouts of stubble on his square chin. "But everyone calls me Xander. Not Alex. I don't like that."

Briefly, I wonder who ever called him Alex.

"And you?"

I take a deep breath as I place my hand in his a second time.

"Robyn."

Xander smiles as he shakes my hand and gives it a little squeeze. I wince at the pressure.

"Ouch." I look at my hand.

It's not bleeding anymore, but the cut is still there, and the skin around it is red and tender.

He frowns. "Maybe we should go inside and take a look at your wounds."

I look down at my feet. "Only after that shower you promised. And clothes. Oh, and that coffee."

Chapter Two

Xander

The gurgling of the water in the coffee machine accompanies my thoughts as I lean on the counter.

Robyn, huh?

A nice name for what seems like a nice person, which makes me wonder all the more—what was a woman like her doing in the back of one of my trucks?

The black and silver machine beeps just as the door to the bathroom opens. I pour two cups of coffee and set them on the table by the window where the sandwiches I've prepared are already waiting.

She stands in front of the mirror I've hung on the wall, pausing in the midst of drying her hair to stare at her reflection.

I, too, find myself staring at her.

Now that her hair isn't tangled and covered in dirt, it shimmers under the light, a river of copper silk. It goes well with the dark blue shirt of mine that she's wearing paired with baggy gray joggers that I unearthed from the bottom of my suitcase. With the ill-fitting clothes on, I can barely make out her long, lean legs, her slender waist or the curve of her firm breasts.

Luckily, I remember them.

"Coffee and food, as promised," I tell her.

Robyn turns around and glances at the table, then walks over to it with the towel still draped around her shoulders.

She sits down, picks up a sandwich and tries to peek at its contents. "What's this?"

"My specialty—pulled pork, cheese, pickles, onions."

She takes a sniff, then a bite. A slice of onion falls on the table and the juice from the pork trickles out the corner of her mouth. She sets the sandwich down and grabs a napkin to wipe it off and pick up the onion.

"Sorry," Robyn mumbles. "I'm a messy eater."

I take the seat across her. "So am I. But doesn't that just mean we enjoy our food too much to care how we look?"

Her full lips, still glistening with oil, curve into her first smile, and her face lights up all at once. Her chestnut brown eyes gleam and her cheeks finally show some color.

I can't help but smile in turn.

She picks up the sandwich again. "You made this?"

I nod. "Like I said, it's my specialty. Or in other words, the only thing I'm good at making."

Robyn gives a low chuckle then takes another bite.

I tap my fingers on the rim of my mug. "How is it?"

She gives me a thumbs-up—her mouth is too full to speak—then takes another bite before setting the sandwich down.

She must be hungry. Of course she is. Joel said he was on the road for nearly sixteen hours, and we didn't open the back of the truck until ten this morning.

She grabs her cup of coffee and takes a sip. Afterwards, she closes her eyes and inhales. She lets the air out slowly and her lips purse together as a murmur of pure contentment travels up her throat.

The expression conjures a different scenario in my mind, and a ripple of excitement travels up my spine.

"I can't tell you how good that is," she says when she finally opens her eyes.

I shift in my seat and hide my heated gaze behind my mug of coffee.

"Isn't it strange how the most pleasure comes from the simplest things?" Robyn asks as her shoulders bunch up. "A cup of good hot coffee. A shower and a bar of soap. Clean clothes. Good food."

Pleasure. I suddenly have the urge to teach her what that's all about.

"We take them for granted too often," she adds. "Just because they're always there. But we need them."

"Ironic," I agree as I set down my mug.

Just as we avoid talking about the most important things.

That ends now.

I clear my throat. "So, how did you end up in the back of my truck?"

Robyn takes another sip of coffee, then looks at me with arched eyebrows. "Your truck?"

I sit back. "Well, it belongs to the company, but the company belongs to me, so yeah."

"The company belongs to you?" Robyn's eyes grow wide.

"Now it does," I answer.

Last year, my uncle officially handed the reins over to me.

"Wow." She nods. "That's amazing and kind of unbelievable. I mean you're so young, and well, you don't strike me as someone who owns a whole company."

"It's not a big company," I tell her.

She bites another chunk off her sandwich and shrugs. "Big. Small. Same thing. It's the position that counts."

I cross my arms over my chest. "You think so?"

"Shouldn't you be wearing a suit or something? Or have a personal assistant to make the coffee and stuff?

Shouldn't you be more... bossy, you know, like high and mighty?"

"I'm not sure who you're imagining, but that isn't me."

"Yeah, I guess." She brushes strands of her hair aside before taking another bite. "So what kind of company is it exactly?"

I frown. Wasn't *I* supposed to be finding out more about *her*? So far, I've dished out a fair amount of information and received none.

"We build vacation homes," I answer briefly. "And what about you? What do you do?"

"You mean aside from showing up naked in the back of trucks?"

I lean forward. "Well, I must admit I'm curious as to how that happened."

I have a few theories, but I'd like to hear the facts from her.

"Especially the naked part, I bet."

Well, I am curious about that. People normally don't go around naked, and even robbers leave their victims with at least the clothes on their backs.

No. Something tells me she wasn't robbed.

"You don't strike me as a nudist," I say as I tap my fingers on the table.

Robyn chuckles and takes another bite of her sandwich. This time, some strands of her hair get in the way and end up in her mouth. She pulls them out and examines the mayo-covered strands with a frown.

I get out of my seat and gather her hair back.

"Hair isn't one of the ingredients in my sandwich, mind you."

The tendrils feel even softer against my palms than I expected. The minty citrus scent of my shampoo, strangely more distinct on her than on me, drifts into my nostrils.

As I pull up her hair, I glimpse the smooth skin of her nape and my pulse quickens.

I tear my gaze away from it and pull a rubber band out of my pocket. Lately, I seem to have a supply on me.

Robyn glances over her shoulder and presents me with an open palm. "I'll do it."

I hand her the rubber band and give her room to tie her hair, but after just twisting it once, she lets out a cry.

"Ow!"

I grab her hand and stare at the reddened cut on her palm.

"We should put a bandage on that."

And by we, I mean me. I head over to the cupboard where I keep my medical kit and fetch it.

I set it on the table and open the jar of cotton balls. I soak one in antiseptic and press it against her palm.

"Ow!" she cries out again.

I take off the cotton ball and grab a Band-Aid.

"Care to tell me how you got this cut?"

"A branch," Robyn explains vaguely.

I stick the bandage across her palm. "You were in the woods?"

That would explain the dirt.

She nods.

"And I'm guessing this was caused by a branch, too." I touch the cut on her cheek.

She flinches.

"What were you doing in the woods?"

"Running."

"From?"

Robyn doesn't answer, but her silence confirms that she was running away from someone. If it had been a wild animal, she would have said it out loud.

The question is: Who was chasing her?

I don't press the issue. Instead, I continue treating her wounds, trying to gain what information I can from them.

Multiple scrapes and bruises. She fell.

Some of the bruises on her arm are older and in the shape of finger pads. Someone grabbed her. Hard.

A cut on her other arm, also older and deeper than the rest, stands out as well. I don't need my paramedic training to tell me that it's from something narrow and sharp.

A whip?

I frown. Robyn may not have told me anything about what happened to her, but my instinct tells me there was a man involved. A father just like mine? No. He would beat her up, but he wouldn't strip her. A sick boyfriend, probably, maybe one on drugs or alcohol or both. Maybe she didn't have her clothes on because she escaped just after he fucked her. Something tells me it was without her consent.

The anger that simmers in my gut and rises all the way to my throat takes me by surprise. My fingers tighten around a tube of antibacterial ointment and its contents spurt out on the table.

"Shit."

I quickly put the cover back on the tube, toss it inside the medical kit and clean my mess up with a paper towel.

"Are you sure you're not a doctor?" Robyn asks.

I shake my head. "I've told you my job, and you still haven't told me yours."

"Wait a minute." She raises a finger. "I thought you were a cop."

My eyebrows arch. Me? A cop? Where did Robyn get that idea?

Then I see the crumpled black shirt on the stool and I understand.

"Nope." I shake my head. "I'm not a cop."

She glances at the shirt. "But that..."

"...belongs to an old friend of mine," I finish the sentence for her.

"Oh."

Robyn's face falls along with her hands, which land as fists on her lap. For a moment, she remains silent. Then she stuffs what's left of her sandwich inside her mouth, takes a few gulps of coffee, wipes her mouth crudely with a napkin and stands up.

"Thank you for everything." She bows her head slightly. "I will surely repay your kindness when I can."

My eyebrows crease. Is Robyn leaving?

It certainly looks like it now that she's heading to the door.

Unbelievable.

"Robyn, wait!"

I can't let her leave, not when there's no guarantee she'll be alright. What if that scumbag she was running away from finds her? What if he begs her to come back to him and she gives in, being the nice person that she is, which I've seen happen too many times before? What if he puts her in chains then? Or what if he beats her to a pulp on sight because he can't forgive her for leaving him?

No. I can't let her leave.

I stand between her and the door. "Like I said, my friend's a cop. He can help you. I can still help you."

Robyn looks at me. "You've helped me enough, Xander. I have to go."

"And where will you go, hmm?"

She doesn't answer.

I grit my teeth but quell my impatience. "Don't you need money to travel? Not to mention shoes?"

I glance at her bare feet.

Robyn looks at them, too, and twitches her toes. "I'll stop by a Payless shoe store."

"With what money?"

She touches her ears, and for the first time I notice the ruby studs on them. "I'll sell these. I'm pretty sure they're real."

Okay. So she has that figured out. Clever.

"Xander..."

I bar her path with my arm. "The nearest bus stop is an hour away, maybe more."

"So you'll drive me?" Robyn asks hopefully.

"Too busy," I answer. "But I can lend you my phone and you can call someone to pick you up."

She quietly looks away.

Just as I thought. She has no one to call.

"Surely your family's worried about you, too," I add.

"They would be if they hadn't died when I was nineteen," she says.

I frown. I suspected she no longer had a family. But to have lost them so recently? And all at the same time?

The expression of anguish on her face grips my chest. If anything, knowing that she has no family has made me want to protect her even more.

"I have to go." Robyn tries to walk past me.

I grab her shoulders. "You're not going anywhere."

She looks at me in surprise, then glances at my hand on her shoulder.

Fuck. Now she thinks I'm like that scumbag who couldn't let her go.

I quickly take my hand off and rub the hair on my nape. "What I mean is that you should stay until you have a better plan."

"A better plan?"

Speaking of which, I've suddenly come up with one.

"Why don't you stay here until our work is done? We only have about two weeks left, and we need someone to cook. You know how to cook, right?"

Robyn nods.

"And maybe do the laundry."

Her eyes narrow. "Would you like me to scrub your backs while you bathe, too?"

"Of course not," I answer quickly. "And I'll pay you. Generously. That way, you'll have enough money to get a new start."

She touches her earring.

"Aren't those earrings valuable to you?"

The gleam in her eyes tells me I'm right.

She crosses her arms over her chest. "How can I be sure I can trust you?"

"If I wanted to hurt you, I would have done it already," I tell her.

She looks at my hands and I raise them in the air. "I won't lay a finger on you, I swear. In fact, I've sworn off women."

She throws me a puzzled look. "Have you, now?"

"And I promise everyone here will treat you with respect." I put my hands down. "They may not smell good most of the time, but they have manners and they'll do as I say."

Robyn looks unconvinced.

"And if at any time you no longer feel safe here, you're free to leave," I add. "I'll drive you to the bus stop myself."

That seems to do it. Her shoulders ease up. Her arms drop to her sides.

"You give me your word?" she asks.

I offer her my hand as I nod. "We can shake on it."

For another moment, Robyn hesitates. Then she takes my hand. I shake hers and smile.

"Well, I do feel like I want to have more of your pulled pork sandwiches," she says with a smile of her own.

"You can have them," I inform her. "My men are tired of them."

"Then I'll make them something better."

I stroke my beard. "I can't wait to see you try."

Again, her brown eyes turn into slits beneath furrowed eyebrows. "Is that a challenge?"

"I'll get you clothes, too."

Robyn shakes her head. "You don't have to."

"I think I do," I tell her. "It's my job to see to it that all my employees are well-equipped to do their jobs, and I think you'll work better with proper clothes. Besides, I'm short on clothes as it is, so I can't lend you more of mine."

"Fine." She sighs, then gives me a salute. "If you say so, boss."

Boss? I've been called that many times before, but it sounds different coming from Robyn. Weird.

"You are my boss from now on, right?"

I pat her shoulder and smile. "Yeah. Welcome aboard."

~

"You asked her to stay?" Joel stops in the middle of smoothing a panel of wood with a chisel to look at me like I'm crazy.

"I told her, actually."

Joel shakes his head as he goes back to his work.

I frown.

Joel was my uncle's right hand man for years, and now he's mine. He's quiet but dependable, hard-working, honest, wise. If he disapproves of something I do, it must be because I'm doing something wrong.

"I couldn't just let her go," I explain to him. "You saw her."

"Yeah, I did." Joel nods. "She's a woman, and you've been without a woman for a long time. Maybe too long."

"She's not just any woman."

"Yeah. She's quite pretty, isn't she?"

"That's not what I meant."

"And she's hurt. And lost. Just your type," Joel adds. "You've sworn off women, but you still can't stay away from the wounded ones."

I sit on the stool across him. "You know me too well."

He looks at me. "Do you really want to do this, though? You're not a hero anymore, Xander."

"I never thought of myself as one."

"And you can't save everyone."

I nod. "Believe me, I know."

I know it all too well. Not a day goes by that I don't look at myself in the mirror, see the scar on my forehead and not remember.

"Still, you want to save her?" Joel asks.

"It's not like I sought her out," I tell him. "Of all the trucks she could have jumped into, she gets into the back of mine."

Joel chuckles, then walks over to me and squeezes my shoulder. "Well, I didn't think a thirty-year-old stud like you would be celibate for long."

"Hey." I nudge his arm. "I'm not touching her."

He pats my shoulder. "Keep telling yourself that."

"Not unless she asks me to."

Another chuckle. "And when has a woman ever not wanted you to touch her, hmm? Just do me a favor and promise me she won't distract you from your work."

"She won't," I assure him.

I may have decided to take Robyn under my wing, but I'm not letting her into my heart, much less letting her get a hold of me.

I've learned my lesson.

Women. You've got to own them or they'll own you.

"She'll need clothes, won't she?" Joel asks.

"She's wearing mine, but yeah, she needs her own. Do you happen to have any of Shannon's?"

"Now, why would I be carrying my wife's clothes?"

"Think you can ask her to send some for Robyn then?" I ask.

"Why don't you just get her clothes online?" Joel suggests. "There's no mall around here, but we do have internet, thank goodness. And I'm sure FedEx will at least be able to find us."

I stroke my chin.

That idea's not half bad.

"Oh, if you're having something shipped, why not get Nash a present, too. His birthday is next week, you know."

"I know." I nod and clasp my hands together. "Maybe we'll throw him a party."

Joel puts his hands on his hips. "Party or no party, something tells me things are going to be livelier around here from now on. After all, it's not every day we've got a girl on the run with us."

I have to agree.

Chapter Three

Robyn

The morning sun kisses the ground through the gaps in the tree canopy, one golden puddle just inches from my hand. A bird chirps on a branch. A soft breeze touches my cheeks and blows the strands of hair that have escaped from my ponytail.

Just yesterday, I was in the woods running for my life. Now, here I am in another forest—doing yoga.

I take a deep breath as I stare at the ground. I'm on my hands and knees. The tip of my ponytail dangles past my shoulder and the neckline of my shirt hangs down far enough that if I look, I can see the tops of my breasts.

I close my eyes, exhale and raise my knees so that my legs are straight but slanted. I lean on my toes before pulling my knees closer to my head so I can rest on my heels, the soles of my feet flat against the ground.

I breathe in and out as I hold my head between my arms. I take in the cool air, the scent of wood and grass. I hear the rustle of the leaves and will the calming force of nature to wash over me.

Breathe in. Breathe out.

I hold the position for about two minutes, careful not to put too much weight on my injured palm. The cut looked better when I changed the Band-Aid this morning, but it's still healing. My whole body is.

Slowly but surely.

When I've finished playing Queen's 'Lazing on a Sunday Afternoon' in my head, I let my knees, arms and forehead fall to the ground in a child's pose. It's a pose of surrender, which in my opinion is the only way one can be at rest.

As I remain curled on the ground, resting, my thoughts drift to Xander.

He's nice. I'll give him that much. But I'm still not sure I can trust him. After all, Howie was nice, too, in the beginning. The jerks all are.

For a moment, I wonder if I should have run when I had the chance. Then I tell myself I've made the right decision in staying.

As much as I don't like admitting it, Xander's right. I need a better plan. Heck, I need *a* plan. And yes, I need money, and if I have a chance to earn it without selling the earrings that my mom bought for me when I was sixteen, I'll take it.

When I've rested my arms and legs long enough, I lift my head. I open my eyes and prepare to strike another pose. This time, I let my back lie flat on the ground while my knees remain folded beneath me. My arms rest at my sides.

Rafts of windswept clouds floating across a blue river appear before my eyes just above the green barrier.

The sight remains in my mind even after I close my eyes. I lift my back and tuck my arms in as I slide my palms beneath my buttocks. As I inhale, I lift my back even further off the floor and rest on my elbows and my lower arms. The top of my head touches the ground.

In. Out.

"Is this a bad time?"

My eyes fly open, then grow wide as saucers as I see Xander's face. Even upside down, it holds me captive for a moment, but I manage to break free and spring upright. One of my hands goes immediately to my neckline to pull it up and press the cotton against my skin—although it might already be too late. I wipe the dust off the other on the back of my pants as I glare at Xander.

"I guess it is," he says as he stands up.

I cross my arms over my chest. "What are you doing here?"

"Finding you," Xander answers. "You weren't at the site, so I was worried you might have run away."

"After I told you I'd stay and we shook hands on it and all?" I shake my head. "I'm a woman of my word."

He grins. "Then that's another thing we have in common."

"Aside from?" I ask curiously as I sit on a log.

Xander scratches his chin. "Liking pulled pork sandwiches?"

I chuckle.

"And wearing the same clothes," he adds as he sits beside me.

I glance at the shirt I'm wearing. "Yeah. They're surprisingly good for yoga."

"Oh, that was yoga?"

I nudge his shoulder.

"Just kidding," he says. "You were good."

In spite of myself, my cheeks turn red. I let my hair loose to hide them.

Xander looks around. "It's nice here, isn't it? Serene. Almost otherworldly."

"Yeah," I agree.

"You like the outdoors?" he asks.

I rub my shoulders. "Strangely, everything else that reminds me of my family hurts, but the woods—they remind me of all the camping trips we took, and they only make me smile."

Just like right now.

As I look around the clearing, I can remember the colorful tents we used to put up—orange for Mom, gray for Dad, blue for Wesley, and finally lime green for me. I can almost see the campfire and the sticks of hotdogs or marshmallows hanging over it. I can almost hear the laughter we all shared over Dad's jokes and the screams at the scary stories Wesley loved to tell. Well, the screams were mostly mine; his stories always failed to spook Mom and Dad, although Mom would sometimes let out a fake gasp. I close my eyes and hear Mom singing. I would sometimes sing along, usually with the wrong lyrics just to make Dad and Wesley laugh.

"I don't know what happened to them, but I'm sorry you lost them." Xander's condolence interrupts my reverie.

"Thank you," I tell him sincerely.

He nods. "So you like camping, huh?"

"I used to," I admit. "I haven't done it in ages."

Not since Mom, Dad and Wesley died.

"Well, that's one more thing I know about you," Xander says.

He counts his fingers.

"Let's see. You like pulled pork sandwiches. You like strong coffee. You like yoga. You—"

"I'm an accountant," I interrupt him. "Well, I used to be."

Up until Howie got me fired.

"An accountant who likes to jump in the back of trucks naked and do yoga in the woods." He nods. "You're a weird one."

"Don't forget how I can kill people with a pair of pliers," I remind him.

"Yeah. That was a neat choice for a weapon."

I snort.

"Well, why don't we go camping sometime?" he asks suddenly. "You see, I happen to like camping, too. That's one more thing we have in common."

"Hmm." I rub my chin. "I'll think about it."

Just then, the breeze carries a high-pitched song from a nearby tree.

Xander stands up, and after a few moments of searching our surroundings, his expression turns to one of surprise.

"Well, what do you know?" He places his hands on his lower back. "That's a robin."

"It is?" I get on my feet. "Where?"

Xander gestures with his head and I walk over to him. Once I'm standing right beside him, he leans forward on his knees and points at some branches ahead.

There, on one of the branches, a small bird with a black head and an orange breast sits. As I stare, its tiny yellow beak moves to continue its song.

"A robin," I whisper as I place a hand over my chest, which has suddenly erupted with warmth.

"I'm guessing that's how you got your name," Xander says. "Because your hair is the same color as a robin's breast."

"Yeah." I nod. "Except my name is with a 'y' and not an 'i'."

"And I'm guessing you can sing, too."

"Nah." I shake my head. "I don't sing. Not unless it's in the shower."

"Ha. Another thing we have in common."

Really?

I try to imagine Xander singing in the shower, but instead of just picturing him from the shoulders up belting out a tune while lathering his hair with shampoo, my mind comes up with a complete and detailed image of his body that includes parts I've seen and parts I haven't.

I blush.

"See, we have much more in common than you think," Xander goes on.

I tuck a few strands of hair behind my ear. "It doesn't matter. It's not like we're going to go out or something. I've sworn off men, too, you know."

"You don't say."

I draw a deep breath. "Besides, I'm leaving soon."

"You better not fall for me, then."

The words make my heart skip a beat. Slowly, I turn my head towards him, my mouth open and poised to give a reply, but no words come out. Instead, my heart stops for an entire moment as I gaze into those amazing gray-green-gold eyes. I quickly look away and clear my throat.

"Shouldn't we head back?" I ask, already walking away from him.

"Yeah," Xander agrees. "The boys are already looking forward to lunch."

I keep walking. "Are they?"

"I told you they're tired of my sandwiches."

I clasp my hands together and stretch my arms in front of me. "Well, I'll do my best not to disappoint them."

~

"This is delicious!" Nash, the carpenter who's in his late twenties, exclaims after trying just one spoonful of my dish. "What is it called?"

I chuckle. "Stir-fried chicken and vegetables. It's a pretty simple recipe."

"Simple but tasty," Joel says.

Xander introduced me to all of them earlier so I now know all their names—Joel, the oldest of the bunch; Nash, who has his baseball cap glued to his head except during meals; Aaron, who has his earphones glued to his ears and barely talks; and the newest and youngest guy, Mike, who has long hair tied in a ponytail and a birthmark on his left arm.

Strange. Once again, I'm surrounded by men. But this time, they turn out to be a nice bunch. At least, I'm starting to think they are.

I turn to Xander, who's already on his second spoonful—or is it his third?

"Well?" I ask him.

"It's good," he answers. "But I'm not convinced it's better than my sandwich."

I frown and stick my chin out. "Just wait until dinner."

"Can't wait to see what masterpiece you can whip with a limited pantry," Xander says before putting the spoon back in his mouth.

"Oh, I'm used to a limited pantry," I tell him.

After all, ever since my parents and my brother died, I've been mostly living alone and on a tight budget.

"Then you should do well in a cooking show," Nash remarks.

I shrug.

"Hey!" Joel scolds. "Slow down, will you?"

I turn to Mike, who's sitting across him, busy gulping down his bowl of food.

"I'm not giving you the Heimlich if you choke," Xander warns.

Aaron, too, throws him a disapproving stare.

Still, Mike continues eating until his bowl is empty, after which, to my surprise, he falls to his knees in front of me.

"Marry me."

My eyebrows go up. *What?*

"Quit screwing around," Xander tells him with an edge of annoyance.

I glance at him and find him eating with a frown.

Is he... jealous?

"Get up." Joel pulls Mike to his feet. "You're scaring Robyn."

"What?" Mike protests. "I'm serious. I don't mind spending the rest of my life with someone who cooks food as good as this."

"Don't mind him," Joel tells me. "The food's just too much for his tiny brain to handle."

Mike frowns. "I'm just showing my appreciation. That's all."

"Like she'd marry *you*," Aaron speaks out.

I look at him and blink.

So that's what his voice sounds like.

"Yeah. She's got better taste," Nash teases.

"Why not?" Mike asks. "I'm definitely better than the last guy she was with."

The spoon between my fingers falls on my plate.

How did Mike know? I didn't tell Xander or anyone about Howie.

No. Of course they know. They all saw what I looked like when I first arrived on the site, after all. Any fool with eyes would be able to tell I've had it rough, and it wouldn't take a genius to come to the conclusion that a guy was responsible.

And Mike's right. He *is* better than Howie.

"Hey, just cut it out, okay?" Xander breaks the silence that's fallen on the group. "I swear I'll punch anyone who makes Robyn cry."

Again, the words take me by surprise, but unlike Mike's words, these fill me with a sense of relief, joy even. After all, they're what Wesley would say if he was still alive.

I haven't been looked after for so long that I've forgotten how good it feels. I shouldn't get used to it, though.

"By the way, it's Nash's birthday next week," Xander mentions, probably to break the tension.

Aaron pats Nash on the back.

"I think we should throw him a party," Xander adds.

At that, Mike's frown disappears.

Nash cheers.

I raise my hand. "I'll bake a cake."

Aaron whistles.

Just like that, the friendly, if not festive, atmosphere returns. I smile before I start digging into my lunch.

Just as I thought, this is really a nice bunch. I may not trust them yet, but I'm beginning to think it won't be so bad being around them.

Chapter Four

Xander

Robyn's even breathing and the hum of the air conditioner keep the silence in the living room at bay. Slivers of moonlight slip in through the cracks in the blinds, painting a series of dashes across her curled-up body and shedding just enough light for me to see her.

She has one hand tucked under her pillow. Her other arm, having escaped from the blanket, dangles over the edge of the couch. Wisps of red coat her cheeks. Every now and then, her eyelid twitches.

I grab a stool and place it under her hand so it's not hanging in the air. Her fingers jerk, but she remains still.

I sigh.

I told her she should stay in the trailer's lone bedroom, but she wouldn't have it. In spite of all she's been through, she wouldn't seize the chance for a bit of comfort. I don't know if it was because of pride or mistrust or something else entirely, since she never struck me as shy. Whatever it was, I was torn between admiration and irritation.

Now, it's undoubtedly admiration.

As I stand above Robyn, gazing at her sleeping face, I find myself admiring her resiliency. She seems to have emerged from hell still an angel, not unscathed yet still able to smile and laugh, to hope and live. Heck, she's doing much better than I was.

It's not just admiration, though. As I brush some strands of her hair aside, my fingertips graze against her cheek and something more primitive and more intense pulls at me from the inside. Heat pools in my crotch.

I've seen her like this before—eyes closed and completely oblivious to my presence.

It was just this morning when she was doing yoga. She seemed so entirely at peace that I didn't want to disturb her.

Then there was the fact that she was so completely fascinating that I just couldn't keep myself from watching.

Not only was her body limber as she executed her poses, but her poses were—well, one of them made me want to grab her hips and grind them against mine.

That same urge seizes me now.

I take a step back, but as I do, my eyes fall on her lips. They're slightly parted to let her breaths escape, and my own breath catches. A knot forms in my throat.

Suddenly, Robyn sits up and half the blanket falls to the floor. Her eyes, wide open and brimming with tears, stare blankly through me as if I'm a ghost. Her chest and shoulders rise and fall as she pants. One of her shaking hands clutches at the pillow.

"Hey," I speak softly so as not to startle her. "Are you alright?"

Robyn doesn't answer.

"Robyn." I step forward. "It's alright. It's me, Xander. You're safe in my trailer. Whatever it was, it wasn't real."

Slowly, she turns her glistening eyes towards me. A tear rolls down her cheek.

"Wasn't it?"

This time, the knot forms in my chest, twisting painfully. Unable to answer her question, I simply sit beside Robyn and pull her into my arms. Her head falls against my aching chest. My hand strokes her back.

"It's okay now," I whisper.

Sobs begin to escape her. Her shoulders shudder. Her tears seep into my shirt.

I simply hold her, stroking her back. I have no words to comfort her. I doubt there are any.

Gradually, I feel the rigid muscles of her back relax beneath my palm. Her shoulders let go of their burden as well. Her breathing slows down. Her sobs turn into sniffs.

Then Robyn pulls away and dries her tears with the back of her hand. She blows her nose on a sleeve.

"Sorry," she mumbles as she tucks strands of hair behind her ear.

"For?"

She points at my shirt, which now has snot stains on the sleeve.

"It'll come out in the wash," I tell her.

"And for acting like this." She looks down at her lap and fidgets with the hem of her shirt.

My eyebrows furrow. "What? For acting frightened after a nightmare? You don't have to apologize, Robyn. It's natural. It happens to all of us, even the best of us."

She sniffs and shakes her head. "I wonder if anyone has worse nightmares than the ones I get."

I shrug. "I won't know unless you tell me what yours are."

Now I'm even more curious about what she's gone through. And I want to crush the skull of whoever's responsible.

"Sometimes it helps," I add.

Robyn, too, shrugs. "I don't know about that."

"You can try," I urge her.

She lifts her head to meet my gaze. "What are you doing here, anyway?"

So she still won't talk about it, huh? I scratch the back of my head. Oh well, it was worth a try.

"It *is* my trailer," I remind her.

"Shouldn't you be in your bedroom?" She throws me a puzzled look. "Why aren't you asleep?"

"I was," I lie. "You screamed."

Her eyebrows shoot up. "I screamed?"

I nod.

She scratches the top of her head. "Sorry."

I shake my head. "It's fine. Whatever you need, I'm here."

Those words seem to surprise her. She looks away.

"Do you get nightmares, too?" she asks as she pulls the blanket off the floor.

"Like I said, everyone gets them."

She looks at me.

"I do, too," I give her the answer she's looking for. "I used to have a lot of them."

"About?"

So she won't talk about her nightmare but she wants to know mine? It's unfair, but I guess I'll have to go first.

I draw a deep breath. "Past mistakes."

She spreads the blanket over her legs. "Aren't all mistakes in the past?"

My eyebrows furrow and I scratch my chin. "You know, you have a point."

"Funny. You don't strike me as a person who's made a lot of mistakes, at least not serious ones."

I snort. "Then you're a poor judge of character. I'm not a god, you know."

"I didn't say you were."

"I've made the worst mistakes anyone can make," I tell her. "Unforgivable ones."

"Everyone deserves forgiveness."

Robyn lifts her legs up on the couch and pulls her knees close to her beneath the blanket.

"Are you sure?" I ask her.

"Okay, not everyone. But you do."

"What makes you say that?"

She shrugs. "You're not as bad as you think you are."

"And I think we've already established that you're not a good judge of character."

Still, I can't help but feel a bit happy she has such a high opinion of me.

Robyn pouts and crosses her arms over her chest. "For someone with a phoenix tattoo, you sure don't seem like someone who's risen from the ashes."

I narrow my eyes at her. "You've seen my tattoo?"

She nods.

Of course she has. I did lend her my shirt before.

"It *is* a phoenix tattoo, isn't it?" Robyn asks.

In answer, I turn my back to her and roll my shirt up to my armpits. She turns on a lamp and moves closer to me.

"It is a phoenix."

I nod.

Back then, it seemed like the perfect tattoo. Now, I'm not sure anymore.

Robyn's warm breath blows across my skin.

"Amazing," she says in admiration.

Her fingertips brush against me, tracing the tattoo. Then they stop.

"These are cigarette burns, aren't they?"

"Yeah."

Sometimes I forget they're still there.

"Did you get this tattoo to cover them up?" Robyn asks.

"That's one reason," I answer.

Her fingertips continue their slow and deliberate journey across the canvas of my skin, traveling lower and lower and...

I pull my shirt down and stand up.

"Sorry," Robyn mumbles again. "I..."

"I just remembered there's something I forgot to check." I glance at Robyn over my shoulder. "Go back to sleep."

Without another word or another glance, I leave the trailer. Once outside, I place my hands on my hips and force a deep breath of cool air into my lungs. I allow the rest to wash over my heated skin in hopes of putting out the embers in my veins.

That was close. Dangerously close.

If Robyn's fingers had dipped any lower, I would have lost it. Or if she had pressed her lips against my skin.

Just the thought of it is enough to make me hard.

Again.

Fuck. Joel's right. I've been without a woman for too long.

Far too long.

And Robyn is turning out to be a very interesting woman.

I slap my forehead.

No. I swore I wasn't going to lay a finger on her, and I plan on keeping my word. I'm not going to scare her away. God knows she's scared enough, and she has nowhere to go.

I'm going to keep her safe from everything, even me.

Especially me.

I look up at the quarter moon and sigh.

I guess I'm going to have a lot of sleepless nights from now on.

~

"Whoa. What's with that look?" Nash asks me the next day as I stride into his workshop.

"What look?" I narrow my eyes at him.

"The 'I didn't sleep a wink all night' look," Nash explains as he straightens up.

I frown. I didn't sleep a wink all night, but I was hoping no one would notice. So much for that.

"I had too much coffee," I tell him as I inspect the window frames he's finished.

"Really? Because you look like you didn't have any. Coffee, I mean."

I throw him a warning glance.

He pats my arm. "Listen, boss. We've all seen how you look at her and how she looks at you. If nothing's happened yet, well, it's only been two days and..."

I give him a threatening glare.

"Okay." Nash backs off with arms in the air. "I won't say another word about it."

He runs his fingers across his mouth as if zipping an invisible zipper.

I nod. "Good."

He heads back to his workbench.

"By the way, have you seen her?"

"Who? Robyn?"

I roll my eyes.

"Yeah, actually," Nash goes on. "She was talking to Joel earlier."

My eyebrows arch. "She was?"

What would she want with Joel?

I head out of the workshop to Joel's tent. I don't have to go in and talk to Joel, though, since I see Robyn sitting on a chair outside my trailer, a laptop on her... well, lap.

A midnight blue ASUS VivoBook with a fifteen-inch screen. Joel's.

As expected, she's busy moving on. In fact, she's probably forgotten all about last night, which is well and good.

I approach her and clear my throat.

"Oh, good morning." Robyn glances up at me for just a moment before turning her gaze back to the screen.

"Good morning." I put one hand on my hip. "What are you doing?"

"Oh. I couldn't sleep anymore last night."

Ah. So I'm not the only one.

"So I started looking for something to do. I was about to start cooking when I saw your files scattered around, and while I was fixing them, I saw your financial records..." She looks up. "Sorry. I couldn't help it."

Okay.

"And what did you find out?" I ask curiously.

"One, that you have a lot of money," she answers.

I touch my chin.

"And two, that you're not very good with math or very organized."

"To be frank, neither of those is my forte."

"Thought so." She continues typing. "So I thought I'd help you out by organizing your financial stuff. Like I said, I was an accountant."

"You did say that."

If I had known she was an accountant in the first place, I would have asked her to do that instead of cook and clean and wash clothes.

"I'll still cook and clean and wash clothes, though," Robyn says. "But I can do this. It might help me get my mind off things. Can I?"

She throws me a hopeful look. Not exactly a sorrowful kitten look, but still a hopeful look that I can't say no to.

I sigh. "Of course you can. In fact, I'll be most grateful."

She smiles. "Good."

"And I'll pay you extra."

Robyn purses her lips. "That's not necessary."

"I insist."

I won't let her sway me on this one.

"And one more thing," I add.

"Yup?"

"May I suggest you use my laptop instead? I don't use mine nearly as often as Joel does."

"Oh." Robyn closes the lid of the laptop. "Yeah, sure. I didn't know you had one, but yeah, I think it would be better if I used yours. That is if you don't mind."

I shake my head. "Not at all. Like I said, I haven't been using it, so I think it will be grateful to get turned on once in a while."

Fuck. Did I just say turned on?

"Okay." Robyn nods and purses her lips. "Then I will gladly turn it on and use it, you know, let it do its thing and have some fun."

I exhale. "Great. Then it's all yours."

Chapter Five

Robyn

I guess Xander wasn't lying when he said he didn't use his laptop much.

The silver Dell logo of the laptop with its tilted 'E' still gleams. The 13-inch screen stares back at me without a scratch or a stain, just a few flecks of dust that I dispel with a puff of breath. The keys, which make no sound beneath my fingertips, all have their full letters and symbols on them and hide no lint or crumbs in between. The fan hums smoothly, quietly.

It's a pity, I think, as I place my fingers on the touchpad. It seems like it's one of the best there is.

At the very least, it's better than the one I used to have, which took me three years to pay off. By then, the fan was already whining in protest, the battery was no longer working, the screen had a few permanent scratches, and some of the keys had started to fade. Not to mention that the keyboard had a collection of lint, crumbs and hairs from the neighbor's cat that I sometimes watched over. It had already paid a few visits to the repair shop, too.

Still, I had good times with it—learned new recipes alongside a bunch of worthless trivia, kept track of what went on with the world, played word games, laughed at memes, watched a few movies, listened to music. Good times.

I look out the window and sigh. I wish I still had that laptop. I wonder who does now. I guess I'll never know.

I turn back to the screen and my eyes spot the icon for the music player.

I wonder what Xander listens to.

I click on the icon and browse through his playlist.

Billy Joel. Billy Idol. Green Day. Red Hot Chili Peppers. Coldplay.

I nod.

Not bad at all.

I click on Billy Joel's 'We Didn't Start the Fire' and nod my head to the first few lines before getting to work after the first chorus.

And boy, is there a lot of work to be done. Lots of data to encode. Lots of spreadsheets to fill. Lots of numbers to crunch.

Not that I'm complaining.

This is good. This will help take my mind off the nightmares like the one I had last night. I already have nightmares when I'm asleep. I don't want to have them when I'm awake. Besides, I'm in my element right here.

People are complicated. Numbers are simple.

They're straightforward. They don't lie or pretend to be anything they're not. If you don't understand them, it's your fault, not theirs.

Thankfully, math has always been my forte.

For the next few hours, I hunch over Xander's laptop, knowing that dinner is in the oven and will be ready in time. The clatter of the keys and Xander's playlist serve as the background to my barely audible thoughts.

When my wrists and my eyes start to tire, I stop. I get off my seat and stretch my arms and legs, my fingers too. I rub my eyes and close them for a few minutes. Then I go grab myself a cup of coffee.

When I return, I admire my finished work. So far, so good. I decide to stop for today, so I close the file. The desktop screen appears with all its icons, including the one for the file I've been working on.

There aren't many icons, not nearly as many as I used to have. I had to rearrange them each time I changed my background so that they didn't block anyone's face or anything else important. Most of these are the basic icons which are already there the first time you turn the computer on.

There's only one that catches my attention and piques my interest—a folder vaguely labeled 'Images'. My mouse hovers over it.

I know I shouldn't snoop. But is this really snooping? Xander did lend me his laptop and told me it was all mine.

Still, I glance out the window to make sure Xander is outside before clicking on the icon and then on the first image.

A house. Another house. And another. Maybe they're the houses he built for his clients? They're all elegant, to be sure, all well made just like the one outside that's nearly finished. But I already knew that Xander's good at what he does. He wouldn't make so much money if he wasn't.

Still, one particular house makes me pause and think, mainly because Xander has a few images of it from different angles.

Yup, the exact same house. And he has a drawing of the plans for it, too.

My eyebrows furrow as I press my face closer to the screen.

Is this house for someone special? Why does it seem important?

I go to the next image and pause again. A woman, a slender brunette in a black and brown dress, looks back at me from the screen, two boys of about four and six standing beside her. One of them has the same shade of brown hair as Xander's.

A lump forms in my throat. Is this woman Xander's... wife?

He doesn't wear a wedding ring, but who knows? Maybe they got divorced, or maybe she's... gone? He did say he made unforgivable mistakes in the past, and losing your family sounds like it fits into that category.

At any rate, she must mean something to him, and strangely, that makes my chest feel tight.

Jealousy? No way.

Moving on, I see an image of another woman, this time in a pink dress and with no kids.

My eyebrows arch. A girlfriend? Didn't Xander say he swore off women?

I keep clicking, seeing one woman after another, all different, all dressed differently. My chest tightens even more. The corners of my lips curve into a frown.

Then I see a woman wearing just a black lace bra and a pair of panties, and my jaw drops as my eyebrows bunch up.

"What the...?"

Just then, the door to the trailer opens and Xander comes in.

Shit.

Quickly, I close every open window on the screen, then click on the browser. The homepage pops up just as Xander stands next to the table.

"How's it going?" he asks as he wipes the sweat off his brow.

"Good." I give him a sheepish grin as I put my hands on my lap.

He looks at my screen. "Are you still working?"

I shake my head. "I just finished."

"Finished?" His eyes grow wide in surprise.

"I mean for the day," I clarify. "I just thought I'd browse a bit."

"No problem." Xander taps his fingers on the table. Then his eyes narrow. "Wait. You weren't just watching porn, were you?"

My eyebrows shoot up as I lift my hands. "Of course not!"

"So you were." He points a finger at me and gives me a smug grin. "That's fine. You're old enough, anyway. Was it good?"

I roll my eyes. "I was not watching porn."

"No?"

"I was..." I try to think of a quick excuse. "I was looking for a recipe for Nash's birthday cake."

Xander's expression softens. "Oh."

I let out an inward sigh of relief as I mentally pat myself on the shoulder for the quick thinking.

"I did say I'd bake him a cake," I remind him.

"I know." He touches his chin. "Have you baked a cake before?"

I shake my head. "Nope. I've only ever baked brownies and cookies."

"Then maybe you should do something like a bake test," he suggests.

I nod. "That's not such a bad idea."

"You can make a list of the ingredients and I'll have Aaron buy twice the amount you need when he goes on the supply run tomorrow."

"Okay."

He leans forward. "What kind of cake were you thinking of anyway?"

Again, I try to think of something on the fly.

"What about an applesauce cake?"

~

Applesauce? Check.

Sugar? Check.

Raisins? Check.

Cinnamon? Check.

Cloves?

My eyes go over the table one more time until they spot the green bottle which is all that's unaccounted for.

Check.

I put down my list and let out a sigh of relief.

I have to give it to Aaron. He got all the ingredients I need, plus he got me some clothes, too. From a garage sale that he happened to pass, but hey, it was sweet of him to remember.

I glance down at the red Batman shirt I'm wearing. While it isn't exactly my size, my color or even my style— I'm not exactly a superhero fan—it's better than Xander's clothes. Of course, I'd rather have something like what the women on Xander's computer were wearing, but this will have to do.

I clap my hands together and rub them.

Alright. Time to start.

I add the sugar into the butter and mix it together, making sure the white granules are completely swallowed up by the yellow paste. Then I pour a cup of applesauce in, mixing that thoroughly, too, before adding the flour, baking soda and spices. The added ingredients make the batter twice as big and twice as hard to mix, so I grunt as I hug the bowl to my stomach and move the spoon around.

God, I sure wish I had a mixer.

"I thought you said this was a simple recipe," Xander says as he appears behind me.

"It is, compared to others," I answer without taking my eyes off the batter. "Some cakes have like a hundred ingredients."

"Really?"

"Really." I give another grunt.

"Need help?"

His hand goes over mine and I stop mixing.

I set the bowl down on the counter and step back. "Okay. You mix."

Xander grabs the spoon and picks up where he left off. He's much faster than I was, and the ingredients soon begin to meld into one.

"Wow." I give a whistle. "You're good at this."

But of course he would be. I mean, look at those muscles. They seem to have expanded and hardened in a matter of seconds.

"Is this good enough?"

I quickly shift my gaze from his muscles to the batter, which has turned a pale brown color. "I think it needs to be mixed just a little more."

"Okay."

He continues mixing, but this time he goes too fast and drops of the batter end up splattering on my shirt.

"Hey!" I frown as I look at the added design on my shirt.

"Sorry," Xander mumbles.

I sigh. "This was a new shirt."

He throws me a puzzled look. "I thought Aaron got it at a garage sale."

I pout and put my hands on my hips.

"Besides, it looks better now. Now the bat looks like it's got eyes."

"It's not supposed to," I tell him.

"You know, I've got an idea." He lifts the spoon out of the bowl.

"Wait a sec." I step back with my hands in front of me. "What are you doing?"

"Making your shirt look better?"

I give him a warning glance. "Oh no you don't."

He holds the spoon coated in sticky batter and comes closer.

"No!" I shriek as I start to run.

He grabs my arm and pulls me back. As he does, the spoon in his hand comes in contact with the front of my shirt, leaving a large smear.

"Oops," Xander mutters.

"Oops?" I look at him with creased eyebrows.

Quickly, I look around and spot the bag of flour.

"You're gonna pay for that."

I grab the flour.

Xander steps back. "Now, now, don't—"

I throw a handful at him. He turns his back to me so most of the white powder lands on his hair.

"What do you know? White looks good on you," I tease.

"It does?" He scoops some of the batter into his hand. "Maybe brown will look good on you."

Laughing and squealing, I run out of the trailer. I manage to make it out, but the batter in Xander's hand still lands on my back. I keep running.

I head to the woods and hide behind a tree, leaning on the trunk to catch my breath.

When I hear a twig snap, I turn my head to see where Xander is—only to have him place a dollop of the batter right on the top of my head. Some of it drips down and covers my nose and my cheeks.

I grit my teeth. This isn't funny anymore.

I cross my arms over my chest. "Really?"

"Sorry," he says sincerely as he starts to wipe the batter off me with his hand. "I went too far."

Xander takes off his shirt and wipes the batter off my face.

"There," he says after he's done.

I say nothing.

"Oh, wait. I missed a spot."

He licks his thumb and runs it across my upper lip to gather a drop of the batter there. Our eyes meet and my heart pounds. Heat pumps through my veins.

I step back and Xander withdraws his hand. I look away in the hope that he doesn't notice I'm blushing.

"Are you okay?" he asks.

I nod even if I'm not. My heart is still racing, my skin still warm. And this isn't the first time this has happened. This was what happened last night, too, when Xander had his back turned to me and I was tracing his tattooed muscles.

What on earth is wrong with me?

"Well, I guess we'll have to make another batch of batter," Xander says.

I glare at him. "And whose fault is that?"

"I thought baking was supposed to be messy and fun."

I let out a sigh. My gaze falls to his chest and I look away again.

"You just love taking your shirt off, don't you?"

"Just for you," he answers with a grin.

My eyes grow wide. What?

"Hey, Xander!" Joel's voice pierces the woods. "Can you come check on something for a bit?"

"Yeah, sure," Xander answers. "I'll be right there!"

He smiles at me. "See you later."

He walks off. After a minute or so, I follow after him back to camp. My heart has finally calmed down, but it still flutters when I remember what Xander did and said.

I try to shake it off, though. Just like the remaining cake batter on my copper tendrils, I'm going to wash Xander out of my hair.

Because there's no way I'm falling for a man who, in spite of all his talk of celibacy, has a dozen girlfriends.

Besides, I'm going to leave soon anyway.

Chapter Six

Xander

My jaw clenches in frustration as my glance travels from the watch on my wrist to the entrance of the trailer.

Nash's party has already started. The music is blaring from the pounding heart of the speakers. The fire is crackling. The food, including the cake Robyn has baked successfully, is on the table. The bottles of beer have already been opened. There's a nearly empty one in the hand of the birthday celebrant.

All that's missing is Robyn.

She's been cooped up in the trailer all day, cooking and baking. Then when the FedEx truck finally arrived she got busy rummaging through the contents of the boxes. She even sent me out so that she could try them on.

I haven't seen her since.

I run my fingers through my hair and let out a sigh.

What's taking her so long? Don't any of the clothes fit? Doesn't she like any of them? Or does she like them all and is simply taking her time making up her mind which of them to wear? Well, she is a woman, after all, so...

My thoughts vanish as the door finally opens and Robyn emerges in the pale pink dress with the green silk sash. The sheer sleeves cloud around her shoulders like a pair of tiny wings. The hem reaches past her knees and rustles as she walks. On her feet, she has that pair of all-purpose gray canvas shoes—which I purchased specifically for their versatility—and on her head, her copper tendrils are held captive in a bun with just a few fugitives hanging over her ears.

I frown as I realize I forgot to buy her earrings or any other jewelry. In spite of that, she still looks fine.

More than fine. The dress fits her perfectly, just as I hoped it would. It hugs her slim waist and curves over her firm breasts, made even firmer by the black bra I bought for her. The rosy hue of the fabric shows off her pale skin and the shimmer of her hair.

She's a woman, alright.

"Hey." Robyn gives me a smile as she walks over to me.

"Hey," I return the greeting after swallowing the lump in my throat. "You look..."

And still, I can't find the words to say as I try not to stare at her.

And fail.

"Finally decent?" she suggests as she turns around.

Her skirt billows and I catch a glimpse of the back of her knees.

I wonder if she's wearing those black panties that match her bra underneath those layers of silk and chiffon. I wonder if they fit her perfectly as well.

"Well?" Her eyebrows arch.

"I'm not sure that's the word I'm looking for," I answer. "But I like what you did to your hair."

Robyn lifts a hand to smooth the top of her head.

"And the dress looks good on you."

She takes a step forward. "You're only saying that because you chose it."

I nod. "That's one reason."

She looks down at her dress and lifts the sides of the skirt. "Well, you did choose well. Then again, I suppose you've had practice."

"Practice in shopping for women's clothes?" My eyebrows furrow.

Robyn places a hand on my arm as she leans forward. "Now, now, Xander, don't be shy. You've shopped for your girlfriends before, haven't you? In fact, this dress was just like the one you bought for an ex, right? Can't say I like the thought, or that it looks better on me than it did on her, but beggars can't be choosers, right?"

I tear my gaze away from the cleavage peeking out of her round neckline. "You're not making any sense."

"All the clothes you bought for me," she says. "You've seen them before, right?"

"Well, yeah," I tell her. "On the website."

This time, it's Robyn who looks confused.

I scratch my chin. "And I can't say I agree that the dress looks better on the model than on you. It looks like it was made for you."

"Model?" Robyn steps back. "She was a model?"

"Weren't they all? That's their job, right? To model clothes?"

She lifts a finger. "So you're saying those women on your computer...?"

"Oh, you saw the pictures?"

Her eyes grow wide. "I didn't mean to. I..."

She stops as she looks away. Her cheeks glow red.

Ah. Now I get it. She saw the pictures of those women wearing different clothes while she was working on my laptop, and she thought they were my exes.

No wonder she looked guilty that time I barged in on her. I knew she was up to something.

I place my hands on my hips. "Seriously, you thought I kept pictures of my exes on my computer? And not even in a password-protected folder?"

Robyn shrugs.

"And let me guess." I lean forward so I can whisper in her ear. "You were jealous?"

"No," she protests quickly. Way too quickly. "Why would I be?"

Good question.

"Well, for the record, no, they're not my exes. And to answer your other question, I haven't gone out with anyone in a while. I've sworn off women, remember?"

She throws me a puzzled glance. "I don't remember asking that."

A whistle from behind me interrupts our conversation. I turn my head to see Aaron with his lips puckered. Mike, on the other hand, has his mouth gaping open just like his eyes.

Nash blinks. "I know I'm not that drunk yet, so I'm not seeing things, right? There's a chick in our camp?"

I'm not sure I like the word 'chick' being used to describe Robyn.

"Happy birthday, Nash." Robyn goes over to him and gives him a hug.

I frown. "Haven't you greeted him a dozen times already?"

She looks at me. "Well, not in this dress."

"It looks amazing." Mike stands up. "You look amazing."

My frown deepens.

Joel walks over to me and gives me a pat on the shoulder at the same time that he hands me an opened bottle of beer. "You should have bought her pants."

I say nothing. I just grab the bottle and take a few gulps.

"Aw. You guys are so sweet," Robyn gushes with a wide smile.

"Well, we're just telling the truth," Mike says as he rubs his nape. "At least, I am."

"Are you calling me a liar?" Nash asks.

Mike ignores him. "Now I feel like giving you flowers."

And I'm pretty sure that's not all he feels like giving her.

Josh chuckles. "What? Haven't you seen a woman in a dress before?"

Mike's eyes remain glued on Robyn. "Not like this, not..."

I clear my throat. I've had enough of this.

"I believe the last member of our party has arrived, so let's not keep the food waiting, shall we?" I walk forward and stop by Robyn's side. "Let's eat."

~

"This food is the most delicious I've ever tasted," Nash says as he licks his fingers.

An empty plate, one that was earlier heaping with pesto spaghetti, baked Buffalo wings and slow-cooked cheese-crusted pork chops, rests on his lap.

I nod in agreement as I toss a clean chicken bone into the pile.

"You've really outdone yourself this time," I tell Robyn.

She smiles. "Thanks."

"Are you sure you're an accountant and not a cook?" I ask.

"You're an accountant?" Mike's eyes grow wide.

"Was," Robyn corrects.

"Anyway, this is the best present ever," Nash says as he puts his plate away. "I can't thank you enough."

"Thank Xander." Robyn points to me. "He's the one who bought the ingredients. I just cooked them."

"I thought I bought the ingredients," Aaron says.

Robyn looks at him in amusement and nods. "I stand corrected."

"Hey, I haven't given you my present yet." Mike takes a package wrapped in brown paper out of the pocket of his jacket. "Happy birthday."

"You didn't have to," Nash says even as he takes the present.

"Open it," Robyn urges.

Nash does. He peels off the brown paper to reveal something small and shiny.

Nash frowns as he holds it up. "Nail clippers? Your nail clippers?"

"Well, you always borrow them, so I thought I'd just give them to you."

Robyn chuckles.

"Well, thanks, I guess." Nash slips the clippers inside his pocket.

Mike frowns. "You guess?"

"And here's my present." Joel hands Nash what looks like an ashtray made from stained glass. "Sorry I wasn't able to wrap it."

"You made that?" Robyn asks in awe.

Joel nods.

"Thanks." Nash pats Joel on the back. "I'll add it to my collection."

"Nash collects ashtrays," I explain to Robyn.

"Well, that's definitely more impressive than my present," she says.

"I'd say they're tied," Nash says.

"Hey," Mike protests. "What about my gift?"

I stand up. "I haven't given mine, either."

Nash looks at me in confusion. "I thought this party was your gift, boss."

"Not quite," I tell him. "Look inside the workshop."

"Okay." Nash enters the workshop. "Are these... tents?"

"Yup," I answer.

"Well, thanks, but..."

"Now, wait in the workshop and hide in there while I get the rest of your presents."

"There's more?" Mike asks before Nash can.

"Okay." Nash disappears further inside the workshop.

I drive away in my Expedition and return minutes later with a load of passengers.

"You can come out now," I instruct as I open the door of the vehicle.

Melanie, Nash's wife, hops out, followed by his two-year-old son, Damien.

Nash gapes. Robyn gasps.

Melanie and Damien run to hug Nash as his sister Nina, his brother-in-law, and finally, his mother, Helen, come out of the Expedition.

"Happy birthday, son," says Helen.

I watch as she gives the teary Nash a tight hug.

"Oh, Mom," he says with a sniff. "I can't believe you're here. I can't believe you're all here."

"We wouldn't miss your birthday," Nina says.

"Wait." Nash pulls away from his mother. "Are you guys all staying here?"

He glances at me and I nod. "That's what the tents are for."

"Yay!" Damien jumps up and down.

I walk over to the MP3 player connected to the speakers to find my favorite song by Guns N' Roses. I tap it and reach for the knob to increase the volume.

"Now that the gang's all here, it's time to get this party going!" I shout over the first notes of the song.

"Yeah!" Nash shouts as he picks up his son and starts dancing.

I smile. I suppose he likes my present.

"Have I ever told you that you're a good boss?" Robyn asks as she joins my side.

"Not that I can remember."

She glances at Nash, who is now dancing with his wife, and lets out a sigh. "This was the best thing you could have done for him."

"Well, this is the first time he's spending his birthday away from home," I say. "We aren't usually busy this time of year."

Robyn turns to me and I meet her gaze. Her eyes gleam softly.

"What?" I ask her.

"Nothing." She looks away.

"I guess now the best present is a tie between yours and mine," I say.

Robyn shakes her head. "I don't even come close."

I nudge her shoulder. "Don't say that."

She says nothing, her eyes back on Nash and his family as she grips one arm.

She must miss her own family.

I grab her hand. "Care to dance?"

Robyn seems surprised at first, but she nods. "Okay."

I place one hand on her hip and pull her away from the speakers, then close to me. Our fingers entwine. Her hand rests lightly on my shoulders. Her breasts threaten to brush against my chest. I smell the alcohol on her breath and hold my own.

For a moment, we remain silent and barely breathing as we move in unison to the music, her eyes lost in mine.

She breaks the gaze first. I break the silence.

"Are you enjoying the party?"

Robyn nods. "I've been to a lot of parties, but I've never quite enjoyed myself like tonight."

I'm suddenly curious to know what parties she's been to.

"It just goes to show that free alcohol, no matter how much, isn't enough to make people happy," she adds with an edge of regret. "It just makes them forget. But then they end up forgetting too much. Sometimes they even forget they're human."

My grip involuntarily tightens on her hip as my jaw clenches. No, whoever hurt her can't be human, which is why it won't be a problem getting rid of him.

It's just pest control.

"So, is there a reason why?" Robyn asks.

"Why what?" I ask her.

"You swore off women?"

Ah, she's changed the topic.

I shrug. "They started to bore me."

"Wow," she says. "There must have been a lot of women."

"None like you," I say without thinking.

Robyn looks up at me with cheeks the same shade as her dress. The same heat erupts in my chest. My gaze falls on her parted lips.

She looks away again. "I'm sure they were taller and prettier than me."

"What makes you think so?" I ask curiously as I try to ignore the heat that's slowly but surely spreading throughout my body.

"Because, well, you're..." She pauses.

I wait for her to continue.

"Hot," she finally finishes.

So the attraction is mutual. Just as I thought.

I tuck the loose strands of her hair behind her ear. "None of them had the same effect on me as you."

"Me?"

I pull her body against mine. Her breasts squeeze against my chest. My inflamed crotch presses against her thigh.

Robyn lets out a gasp and pulls away, runs off towards the trailer and goes inside. I follow her and lock the door behind me.

"What are you doing?" Robyn whirls around, panting.

"Nothing yet," I tell her hoarsely.

She shakes her head. "We can't do this, Xander. I barely know you."

"You know me enough," I tell her.

"I'm leaving soon."

"All the more reason to seize the moment." I step forward and touch her burning cheek.

"You've sworn off women, remember?" she reminds me.

"And you've sworn off men," I answer. "So what? That only means we both need a good fuck. A real one."

She swallows. Her lips quiver.

"Robyn," I whisper her name just before I seal her mouth with mine.

Chapter Seven

Robyn

I stagger back from the weight of Xander's lips. His arm goes around my back to keep me from falling, holding me close. My heart pounds.

At first I think of resisting. Every alarm in my body is going off. A siren blares inside my head.

But at the same time, every vein beneath my skin is on fire, every nerve on alert. My breasts swell against his chest. My nipples tingle.

Xander is right. I do need this.

I need to know how it feels to be fucked by a real man.

And I want to.

The wet spot in my new panties seconds the motion.

I clutch the front of Xander's shirt, close my eyes and press my lips against his. Then I part them so that his tongue can slide in.

The traces of alcohol in his mouth go straight up to my head and make it spin. The heat goes straight down to my belly and between my legs, where the strip of fabric being held captive there grows even wetter.

The hand on my cheek slides down to cradle my jaw. The tongue in my mouth wanders and conquers as my own flails around.

A moan vibrates in my throat.

When Xander pulls away for air, I open my eyes. They stare right into his, which seem to be all aglow, more gold now than green. They take away what breath I have left.

He grips my neck and kisses me again. My back finds the wall. My hands slide down to his hips.

As our tongues entwine anew, his hands move to my shoulders and then lower, past my armpits and down my sides. His thumbs venture dangerously close to my nipples and my heart stops. A shiver descends across my spine.

His hands move to the back of my dress. His fingers search for the buttons and find them. I arch my back to give him space to undo them. Even so, he struggles.

"I should have bought a dress with a zipper," Xander mumbles against my mouth as he finally manages to slip the topmost button out of its buttonhole.

"You should have," I agree. "You have no idea how long it took me to button those."

"I think I do." He gets another button free. "It's a miracle you buttoned them at all."

He struggles with the third button.

"Fuck." The curse escapes his lips as his fingers fumble. "How was I supposed to know this dress had buttons? It didn't say that in the catalogue and it surely wasn't in the picture."

I grin. A man losing his patience to a bunch of buttons. Somehow I find it sexy.

I turn my back to him. "I wouldn't want you to ruin the dress."

"Thanks."

One after the other, the buttons pop out. Then the sash comes undone. The back of my dress opens down to the waist.

I reach for a sleeve to slide it off, but my hand stops as Xander traces the scar across my back.

"This looks old."

"It's from when I was a child," I inform him. "I was on a carousel and it exploded."

"What?"

"Some technical problem."

Xander says nothing. The next thing I know, the tip of his tongue presses against the scar and my hand drops. My knees buck.

As he licks the scarred skin, his hands crawl under the dress and his palms rest on the cups of my bra.

I put my hands on the wall in front of me and throw my head back. A gasp escapes my lips.

With his hands squeezing my breasts through the lace, Xander begins a trail of reverent kisses down my back. The last one marks the spot just above the waistband of my underwear. As his mouth retraces the trail, one of his hands drops down. It brushes against my belly and I tuck it in as I draw a deep breath. My fingers curl and my nails scrape the wall.

Unlike his mouth, his hand does not stop at the waistband of my panties. It slips in. My eyes open wide.

It crawls between my legs and begins to stroke. My hands clench into fists and my knees shake. My toes curl inside my shoes.

Two of his fingers enter and I let out a cry. The heat inside me spills over and the swamp spreads in my panties.

Xander grips my chin and turns my head to his. His mouth swallows my next cry and the one after. They spill out of my mouth even as I overflow on his fingers.

When he breaks the kiss, I turn around to face him. I slip the sleeves off my arms so that the dress droops. I push it down and it forms a puddle around my ankles.

As I kick it aside, Xander's lips find my neck. His fingers lose themselves in my hair and the copper nest unravels.

I place my arms around him. My palms flatten against the cotton as they come in contact with the hard muscles of his back.

Again, he reaches behind me. The hooks of my bra don't put up as much of a fight as the buttons of my dress. It loosens and his hands cradle my breasts. I shiver and grab handfuls of his shirt.

The pads of his thumbs press against my stiff nipples and I let out a moan. He stifles the next one with another kiss. My knees threaten to give way and I cling to him.

When his hands drop to my waist, I manage to recover some of my strength and my capacity for thought. I reach for the hem of his shirt and pull it up and over him. As I let my bra fall, my eyes rest on his bare chest. The strands of hair gleam with beads of sweat under the light creeping in through the blinds. Again, I find myself reeling.

Xander leads me to the couch and I sink onto it. His eyes hold mine captive as he hooks his thumbs into the waistband of my panties. I lift my hips so he can pull them all the way down to my ankles. Then he takes my shoes off and throws them aside with my underwear.

"Careful," I scold. "I like those shoes."

"Sorry," he mumbles. "I'll give you something else to like."

He grabs my thighs, pulls my hips forward and buries his head between them.

My eyes grow wide as I realize what he's about to do.

"Xander, d—"

The rest of the sentence evaporates as the tip of his tongue presses against my nub. My fingers pull at his hair.

Then he moves even lower. His tongue slips in and my jaw drops.

He's... licking me there?

"What's wrong?" he pauses to ask. "Has no one ever done this to you?"

I shake my head. Howie was only ever interested in taking, not giving, even in bed. He was always in a hurry to put his cock inside me.

Xander lifts his head. As our eyes meet, a grin forms on his lips.

Then he spreads my thighs wider and digs in.

Beneath closed eyelids, my eyes roll to the back of my head as it crashes down on the couch. My legs shake and my toes curl. My hips rise off the upholstery.

His tongue slides in and out and I melt like a candy. Heat bubbles in my veins. Knots form in my belly.

His fingers begin to stroke my nub as he continues to lick. The knots begin to come undone.

Then something in me snaps. The bubbles of heat burst and my blood rushes. I lift my arm and let out a cry against my skin. My body quakes all over.

The explosion sucks the breath out of my lungs and wipes every thought from my mind. My arms fall limp at my sides, my strength extinguished.

When I recover, I open my eyes and find Xander standing in front of me, his cock in his hands.

I stare at its engorged tip, at its curved length, at the veins that web around its girth. It's magnificent in every way, just like its owner. My mouth waters and I swallow.

Unable to resist, I reach out to touch it. It throbs against my palm and I feel something warm and wet against my skin. I catch the scent of something sweet and salty and excitement fires up my nerves again.

Strange. I used to hate sucking Howie's cock. Now I want nothing more than to taste this quivering rod of flesh, to worship it. I wrap my fingers around the base and part my lips to let my tongue swipe against the head.

Xander sucks in a breath. I give another lick and he shivers.

I open my mouth wide to take him in, but he grabs my wrist. He pushes me down against the couch. His half lidded eyes, brimming with heat and desire, hover over mine.

"Sorry," he mutters in a whisper, "but I can't wait any longer."

I nod. I still haven't found my voice.

He kneels between my legs and grips my thighs. His cock brushes against one of them and leaves a sticky trail.

I grab his shoulders and hold my breath. He clenches his jaw as he enters me slowly.

His cock stretches me and fills me to the brim. I let out my breath in a gasp and close my eyes.

"Are you okay?" Xander asks.

I nod without opening my eyes. "I'm fine. Just... move."

And he does. His cock slides in and out, rubbing against me. I feel a sting at first, but that fades as I melt around him.

As he picks up his pace, I find my voice—only to lose it again in moans and cries and whispered curses. The springs of the couch creak.

I clutch at his shoulders and throw my head back. My eyes are squeezed so tight tears escape.

"Robyn," Xander says my name just before he gives one last thrust.

I move my hips against his as I ride my second orgasm. It's not as wild a storm as the first, but exquisite pleasure overwhelms my senses just the same.

I squeeze him as he pours himself inside me, his body trembling like mine. My nails dig into his skin.

After he pulls out and gets off me, I watch as he tucks his spent cock back into his boxers and zips his pants up.

"Are you okay?" he asks again.

I nod.

He touches my cheek. "I'm sorry if I was a little rough."

"I'm used to it," I tell him.

Xander frowns as he puts on his shirt.

Ah. It seems the spell has faded.

"Shall we go back to the party?" he asks. "I don't think it's over yet."

So we're just going to pretend nothing happened, huh?

The disappointment causes an ache in my chest that takes me by surprise.

I turn on my side to face the back of the couch.

"You go ahead," I say. "I just need to rest a bit."

"Okay."

After a few moments, I hear the door to the trailer open and close. I remain on the couch, my thoughts racing now that my mind has cleared and my heart has calmed down.

What the hell have I done?

Yes, it was a good fuck, the best I've ever had. Even now, with my body still sore, I want to do it again. But that's precisely why I never should.

I never should have had sex with Xander.

Because now that I know how amazing it is to have a piece of him, it's excruciating not to have the rest.

And I can't have the rest.

I slap my forehead. *Oh, Robyn, when will you ever learn?*

But what's done is done. He's made my body his. I just have to make sure he doesn't do the same with my heart.

I place my hand over my chest.

There's no way I'm staying here—or leaving here without it.

No matter what, I mustn't fall for Xander Bolt.

Chapter Eight

Xander

"What did you do to Robyn?" Joel asks as he rests his elbow on my shoulder.

I shrug, my gaze on Robyn, who at the moment is occupied with measuring a wooden board on a bench. Her hair is coiled in a braid, the last few twists hanging over her shoulder just above the strap of her denim jumper dress. The other strap circles around her arm.

I lift my cigarette to my lips and take a puff.

I know what Joel is talking about. Ever since Nash's birthday party, Robyn has changed.

Well, she still is witty and caring and hardworking, if not more so. What I mean is she's changed towards me.

She never came out of the trailer that night. The morning after, she told me that she couldn't put the buttons of her dress back on and she felt tired so she went to sleep. She spent that whole day with Nash's family. And the next.

At first, I thought she was spending time with them because she missed her own family. But after they left, she started spending her spare time learning the basics of woodworking from Nash, crafting stair railings with Mike, handing Aaron tools, even watching Joel work with glass. When the electricians came, she spent time with them, too, watching them and helping out in every little way she could.

In short, she's been spending time with everyone but me.

I thought I was the only who noticed it, but I should have known Joel would, too. Nothing escapes him.

The question is: Why? All I did was have sex with her.

At the memory of her gasping and trembling beneath me with her hair stuck to her flushed cheeks and her eyes glistening with tears, heat immediately rushes into my balls. My cock quivers in its cotton prison.

Damn. That fuck was even better than I imagined, maybe one of the best I've ever had. I was hoping for a repeat, but I guess that's unlikely.

I scratch my head.

Why is Robyn avoiding me?

"Maybe she wanted to be on top?" Joel suggests. "Or maybe she wanted to cuddle after."

"I don't..." I stop and look at him. "You think I slept with her?"

"I know it," Joel answers with conviction.

I narrow my eyes at him.

"What? You think no one wondered where the two of you suddenly disappeared to, or noticed that you came back alone and with a grin on your face?"

"I was not grinning."

"You were," Joel insists.

I exhale. As I thought, nothing escapes his notice.

"Besides, your trailer was shaking."

My eyebrows furrow. "It was not..."

Joel chuckles.

"Fine," I give in. "I slept with Robyn."

"And?"

"It was amazing," I confess.

Joel gives me a cryptic grin.

"What?" I ask him.

"Nothing," he answers. "If it was as good as you say it was, then something else is the problem."

He squeezes my shoulder.

"And I suggest you find out before we run out of things to keep her distracted. Besides, she isn't going to be around much longer."

I nod. In less than a week, we'll be out of here. That means Robyn will be gone in just several days. I can't let her leave like this. I can't let things end like this.

I extinguish my cigarette beneath the sole of my boot and walk over to her.

"Hey."

"Hey." She looks up for just a second before returning to her work.

I fold my arms over my chest. "You've been busy."

"Yeah. I thought I might as well make the most of my time here. I am leaving soon, after all."

"I know." I step forward. "Speaking of making the most of things, why don't you and I...?"

"Oh, I'm sorry." She tucks a strand of hair behind her ear. "I told Nash I'd help him out this afternoon, and Joel said he'd show me how to put the pieces of glass together tonight."

"Wow." I nod. "You are busy."

Robyn shrugs.

"You do remember that they work for me, right? So they wouldn't mind if I borrowed you."

She shakes her head. "I haven't forgotten. And maybe they won't mind, but I would. I hate breaking my promises."

"You work for me, too," I remind her.

Her eyebrows crease. "Are you ordering me to spend time with you? As my boss?"

I frown. As tempting as that sounds, I'm not sure that's the right approach.

"No," I answer.

"Okay."

She goes back to her measuring tape and her pencil.

I reach for her hand. "Robyn…"

She pulls it away quickly, as if I've scorched her. As she does, the back of her hand scrapes against the edge of the wood. A red line forms on her skin.

"Shit," I curse. "I'm sorry."

Robyn hides her hand behind her. "It's fine."

"Let me look at it."

"It's fine." She walks away. "Just a scratch. I'm fine. You don't have to worry about me."

I grab her wrist. "But I am worried about you."

She turns to face me.

"What's going on? Tell me."

She gives me a puzzled look. "What do you mean?"

I take a deep breath. "Why have you been avoiding me?"

"I haven't…"

"Robyn."

She sighs but doesn't answer, just withdraws her hand and looks away.

"Is this because of what happened the night of Nash's birthday? Was it something I did? Something I didn't do?"

Another sigh.

"Robyn..."

"Fine. I thought I liked you, but after the sex, I don't."

The straightforward answer takes me by surprise.

"You didn't like the sex?"

Robyn shakes her head. "Or you."

Ouch.

"You got what you wanted, right? So please leave me alone."

She turns on her heel and leaves.

For a moment, I just stand there, too wounded and dumbfounded by how the conversation went to move. I manage to recover and pick up the pieces of my shattered pride, though, and I head back to where I left my pack of cigarettes.

"It didn't go well, huh?" Joel asks.

I frown as I grab another stick from the box. "Women. I don't understand them."

~

It's strange, though. I seem to understand Caitlin, our partner interior decorator.

As I help her carry the furnishings of the house and set them down exactly where she wants them, she takes every opportunity to run her hands through her blonde hair, to bend over so that I can glimpse the tops of her breasts threatening to spill out of her low neckline, to brush her body against mine and flash me that gleaming smile of hers.

It's clear she wants to sleep with me, probably just for the thrill of it and so she can brag about it excitedly to her friends.

As Caitlin hangs a picture on the wall, I stare at the butt she's practically wiggling in front of me and consider the prospect.

If there's anything I learned from having sex with Robyn, it's that I need it. If Robyn is unavailable, then maybe Caitlin can fill that need.

Or not.

In spite of all her blatant flirting and her profuse attempts to arouse my imagination and my body, I can't seem to summon any interest. There's no fire in my veins, or my cock.

Strange.

"Is something wrong?" Caitlin turns around and gives me a smile.

"No," I tell her. "Everything's perfect."

"Really?" She walks over to me and stops right where I can look down and see her boobs. "You seem lost in thought."

She places a hand on my shoulder and leans forward to whisper in my ear. "Whatever you need, you know you can count on me."

Just as I thought.

Just then, Robyn enters the room. As her eyes meet mine, she stops. The box in her arms falls to the floor.

Caitlin turns around. "Be more careful, will you? You'll ruin my rug."

"Sorry," Robyn mumbles as she bends down to retrieve the box.

The pliers fall out and I pick them up.

I hand them over to her. "Your favorite tool."

No reaction.

"Wait." Caitlin joins my side. "There's a woman working for you?"

"Yes," I inform her. "This is Robyn. She's my accountant."

"Hi," Robyn says.

Caitlin gives me a puzzled look. "You have an accountant?"

I nod.

"Well, she doesn't have to work here, though, right? Shouldn't she have an office somewhere...?"

"She also cooks for the boys," I say. "And she helps out." I gesture to the box.

Caitlin's hands go to her hips. "Alexander Bolt, you have a woman doing your dirty work?"

"I don't mind getting my hands dirty," Robyn says. "You should try it sometime."

The spite in her voice doesn't escape my notice.

So she doesn't like Caitlin any better than Caitlin likes her, huh?

"No thanks," Caitlin replies as she glances at her nails. "I'd rather dig my hands into something... more delightful."

She glances at me.

"You're wasting your time," Robyn says. "Xander's sworn off women. Didn't he tell you that?"

Caitlin's eyebrows crease. "No."

She looks at me and I nod.

"It's true."

Caitlin shakes her head. "That can't be true."

Robyn sticks her chin out. "He said it himself."

Caitlin steps forward. "That's what he said to *you.* You think you know him, do you?"

"I know him well," Robyn states.

I touch my chin. Well, this is getting interesting.

"You don't know him at all," Caitlin says.

"I know he prefers black underwear on women and you don't have to seem any."

Caitlin gasps.

"And that he sings in the shower," Robyn adds.

Caitlin grits her teeth. "Are you sure you're an accountant?"

"Are you sure you're an interior decorator?" Robyn throws the question back with arched eyebrows.

Caitlin's hands clench into fists.

Alright. This is getting serious now.

I clear my throat and step between them. "Alright, back to work, everyone."

The glaring contest continues.

"Caitlin?"

"I don't want her here," Caitlin tells me.

"Excuse me?" Robyn asks.

"She's ruining my concentration."

"Oh, was that what were you doing?" Robyn asks. "Concentrating? On what, exactly?"

To my surprise, Caitlin lifts her hand. Her palm falls across Robyn's cheek.

I gape. Robyn leaves.

"Robyn!"

I try to follow her, but Caitlin grabs my arm.

"How dare you do something like that?" I ask her. "I thought you were better mannered."

"She started it," Caitlin says.

I shake my head.

"Send her away," Caitlin orders.

I narrow my eyes at her. "You're forgetting who's boss here."

"You're not my boss. You're my partner. We're supposed to respect each other's opinions."

"I'm not sending her away, Caitlin," I tell her. "Especially not for such a petty reason."

"Well, here's a better reason, then. The Overtons are coming over tomorrow to look at the house, and if I remember, they're a very old-fashioned and religious couple. What will they think when they see a woman here with you and all your men?"

I hate to admit it, but she has a point.

I shake off her hold and leave the room.

"Alexander, where are you going?" Caitlin calls after me.

I ignore her as I go after Robyn. I find her outside the house rubbing her cheek.

"Are you alright?" I ask her.

She nods. "I'm used to it."

Again with that. I frown.

"Sorry."

"It's not your fault," Robyn says. "I shouldn't have lost my temper."

Yet she did. Even though she said she didn't like me, what she did in there was clearly an act of jealousy.

"So did your new girlfriend convince you to fire me?" she asks.

"No," I answer. "But I'll need you to stay in the trailer tomorrow when the Overtons come over, just to avoid any trouble. I want them to focus on the house, if possible."

Robyn nods. "Yeah. I understand completely."

So she says. Yet she seems to be in a worse mood. And like before, I don't understand why.

I run my hands through my hair and let out a sigh of exasperation.

Women.

Chapter Nine

Robyn

"Men."

I let out a groan of frustration as I rest my head on the edge of Xander's double-sized bed.

That groan is lost in the hum of the air conditioner which is the only sound in the room. The glow from the screen of the laptop on my crossed legs takes the place of the sunlight that has been barricaded by the tightly shut blinds.

Once again, I'm in a prison.

I stare at the ceiling.

I don't really mind. I understand why I have to stay here, away from the questioning, disapproving eyes of the Overtons. They're seeing their house for the first time, so I mustn't ruin their special moment. Besides, I want them to appreciate all the guys' hard work.

What I don't understand is what Xander sees in Caitlin.

I mean, that woman is a bitch. She has no shame. She has no manners.

I rub my cheek. She slapped, me for God's sake.

So why was Xander flirting with her back in that room? Why was he letting her rub against him and whisper stuff in his ear?

I'm not jealous. Why would I be?

I'm just pissed. I don't like women like Caitlin. I especially don't like how they often get what they want, at least more often than nice women like me.

Clearly, Caitlin wants Xander. I simply don't want her to have him.

I turn my gaze to the screen of Xander's laptop and catch the faint reflection of my fiery hair.

It's not up to me, though. It's up to Xander.

If he allows himself to fall into her clutches, then he deserves her. They deserve each other.

Nope. I'm not jealous.

I put my fingers on the track pad and start searching for interesting information on the web.

News. Depressing as always.

Movie trailers. Nothing new. Either remakes of the classics or superhero movies.

Music videos. Still not as good as the old ones. Too much flesh and not enough intelligible words.

Suddenly, my attention jumps to the sound of running footsteps just outside the trailer. Curious, I set the laptop down on the floor and peek through the blinds. My eyebrows crease as I catch a glimpse of a small red cap disappearing into the bushes.

Who was that?

"Samuel!" I hear a woman shout.

Quickly, I close the blinds and sit on the edge of the bed. Outside, I hear more footsteps and voices as well as the rustling of leaves.

Moments later, I hear a knock on the door.

"Robyn, it's me," Xander speaks from behind it. "Open it."

I open the door. "What happened?"

"The Overtons' son, Samuel, suddenly bolted," he explains as he rummages through the contents of a drawer. "We have to look for him."

My eyes narrow. "Bolted?"

Xander nods as he puts something in his pocket.

"I saw him," I tell him.

He looks at me. "You saw Samuel?"

I nod. "I know you told me not to look outside but I heard footsteps and—"

Xander grabs my shoulders. "Where did he go?"

I pull one of the blinds down and point at the bushes outside.

"He went that way."

Xander frowns, then heads to the door.

"Should I help?" I ask him. "I know you told me I shouldn't let them see me, but that little boy could be in danger. You need all the help you can get."

He nods. "Alright. But put on one of my jackets and a cap so the Overtons don't notice you're a woman."

"Okay."

After he leaves, I grab the green jacket that's draped over a chair and slip it on. Then I reach for the Raiders baseball cap on the wall and hide my ponytail underneath it. I pull the hood of the jacket over my head as well before zipping the front.

I glance at the mirror.

Alright. I don't look much like a woman now. Well, I've never been very feminine to begin with, not like that Caitlin.

I snort and push the image of her in that slutty dress away as I walk out of the room.

I should stop thinking about her, especially right now.

I have to help find that boy.

~

There's still no sign of him.

After nearly an hour of searching through bushes and behind trees that all look the same, I sit on a rock with my shoulders slumped. I take off my hood and my cap and wipe the sweat from my brow.

Where can that boy be?

Just then, I hear the crackle of a leaf. I put the cap back on and look behind a tree. My eyes and my mouth gape open as I finally see a small head of brown hair and trembling shoulders. As the head turns, dark eyes brimming with tears gaze up into mine. One of them has a scratch below it.

"Samuel." I kneel beside him and touch his cheek. "You're hurt."

"I'm fine," he says as he buries his face in his arms.

I'm about to pat his head when I remember something.

"Where's your cap?"

"Lost it," comes the muffled answer with a sniffle.

I take off the cap I'm wearing and put it on his head.

"There. You can borrow mine. Well, it's not mine. It's my... boss's. But I'm sure he won't mind."

Samuel lifts his head and looks at the cap with a frown. "It's too big for me."

"Right now it is," I tell him as I sit beside him. "Because you're still a boy. But you'll grow into a fine man someday."

He doesn't seem convinced.

"How old are you?" I ask him.

"Eight," he answers.

"Then you're practically a man."

The corners of his lips twitch into a smile.

I lean against the tree. "You know, being a man is more than just age. It's about courage, and I'm sure you've been very brave hiding out here all this time."

He hugs his knees to his chest. "It is a little scary."

"Being a man is also about being responsible. Do you know what that means?"

Samuel shakes his head.

"It means not making others worry about you."

"Oh."

"I'm afraid that right now, your mother and father are very worried about you."

He frowns. "No they're not. They don't care about me."

I turn to him. "What makes you say that?"

"They only care about church and about their friends."

"That's not true." I shake my head. "I may not have met your mom and dad, but I'm sure that's not true."

His eyebrows go up. "How would you know?"

"Well, because I had a mom and dad once, and I know that even when they got mad at me, they still loved me."

"Once?"

I clasp my hands together. "I don't have them anymore. I wish I did, though. No matter how old you are, you still need your parents. But they can't stay around forever. That's why you have to be good to them while they're still around."

Samuel falls silent.

I draw a deep breath. "I'm sure if you tell them what's bothering you, they'll help."

He shakes his head again. "They won't. They'll get mad."

I place my arms around my knees. "Well, why don't you tell me, then?"

He looks at me. "Why?"

"Because I'm your friend."

"I just met you."

"Yeah. But I found you. That makes you my friend."

He snorts.

"Go on." I nudge his shoulder. "You can tell me, and maybe I can help you."

He keeps silent.

"Is it about the house? Do you not like it? Because I do. I wish I got to live in it, but you're the lucky one."

"I'm not lucky," Samuel mutters.

"So you don't like the house?" I ask him.

"It's not the house. Just my room. There are angels painted all over the walls and I don't like them. Angels are for girls. Besides, some of them look scary."

I nod.

I remember seeing that room once. I never thought it would be a kid's bedroom.

"Well, maybe your parents just wanted angels watching over you," I tell Samuel. "That's how much they care."

"Well, I don't want the angels," Samuel says in a louder voice. "I'd rather *they* watch over me."

Okay. I think I understand the situation a little better now.

"Well, why don't you tell your parents what design you'd like, and then how about all of you paint your room together?"

Samuel lifts his head, then puts it down again. "They'd never agree to that."

"It's worth a try."

He shakes his head. "They won't understand. They think they're always right."

"No one's always right," I tell him. "And you can't help what you feel. It's not wrong. It's just... you. And you're their son, so they'll understand you."

He hugs his knees tighter. "I'm scared."

"You know what that means? That means you're going in the right direction, because you're stepping out of your comfort zone. You're trying something new, something that can help you become a better you." I reach for Samuel's hand. "It's scary, alright, but you can't let the fear get ahead of you or hover over you forever. You have to put it behind you and move forward."

Samuel gives me a puzzled look.

Right. What I said is probably too much for an eight-year-old. It's simple enough for me, though.

What was that they said? That the best advice to take is often the advice you give?

"I think I get what you're saying." Samuel nods. "If I don't tell my parents then nothing's going to change."

"Exactly." I lift a finger. "You have to take that first step. You'll see, they'll be happy. And because you tried your best, they're bound to try their best to understand you, too."

"You think so?" he asks hopefully.

I nod and place a hand on his shoulder. "I believe so."

I get up and offer him my hand. "Now, let's go and find out if I'm right."

~

"You were right," Xander tells me an hour later as the Subaru Forester leaves the driveway. "I needed all the help I could get, and I'm glad I got yours."

"The Overtons didn't mind that you've got a woman working here?" I ask him.

Xander shakes his head. "They were too happy that you found the boy."

"And did they listen to him? Did they agree to repaint the walls?"

Xander turns to me and nods.

I smile. "It's funny what people can do when they actually try instead of letting fear hold them back."

"Yeah," he agrees.

And if Samuel can conquer his fear, so can I. I can't let the fear of not doing something prevent me from doing it.

I step closer to Xander. "So, did they like the house?"

"Yeah. There are just a few changes that need to be made, a few additions."

"I see."

He tucks his hands inside his pockets. "But overall, they loved it."

"Of course they would. You put so much work into it."

Xander narrows his eyes at me.

"What?" I ask him.

"Nothing," he says. "It just sounded like that was a compliment. And you don't give compliments to someone you don't like."

I purse my lips.

"Is there something you wanna tell me?" Xander asks.

I draw a deep breath. "I lied. The sex was good. You were good. And yeah, I guess I like you."

His thin lips curve into a grin. "Good, because I like being with you, too. I mean, you're the only woman here who gets me."

"I'm the only woman here," I remind him. "Unless you asked Caitlin to set up camp."

Xander snorts. "Like she'd ever agree to that."

I chuckle. "I guess not. She'd be forced to wear underwear so the bugs wouldn't crawl into tight spots. Well, on second thought, maybe not so tight. But anyway, she doesn't seem to like them."

Xander chuckles as well. "And you really don't like her, do you?"

I point to my cheek. "She slapped me."

He nods. "Well, speaking of camping, why don't we go for a hike and camp somewhere for a night? I do believe we said we'd go hiking sometime."

"I think you mentioned it."

"So do you want to? Before we leave?"

I meet his gaze and nod. "Yeah. Why not?"

Like I said, I might as well seize the moment.

Chapter Ten

Xander

I look up into the clear sky and lift my hand to shield my face from the sun. A bead of sweat rolls down my jaw.

I glance over at Robyn and find her fanning her chest with her soaked shirt. Her cheeks glow red, and this time, it's not my fault.

I wipe the sweat off my brow.

We sure chose a hot day to go hiking.

"Do you still have water?" I ask her as I take my bottle out of my backpack.

Robyn nods as she opens hers. "But not enough."

She drinks a few gulps and then splashes the rest on her face. The pearls of water trickle down her face and neck. I follow one as it slips beneath the neckline of her shirt to join the puddle of sweat in the valley between her breasts. Another makes it past the cotton barrier and skims over a soft but firmly rounded curve.

I swallow.

"Hot, isn't it?" Robyn asks as she wipes off the rest of the water and sweat with the back of her hand.

"It sure is," I answer with my eyes still on her.

When she turns her head, I look away and gulp down my water.

"Should we turn back?" she asks. "I sure could use some air conditioning right now."

"I have a better idea." I put the lid back on my water bottle. "Since you're looking for water, I say we stop by the river. It's not too far from here."

"The river?" Her eyebrows arch. "That sounds nice."

I put my water bottle back inside my backpack and offer her my hand.

"Come on."

I lead her up the trail and down some slopes. Leaves rustle as we pass. The crisp ones on the ground crackle.

Finally, I hear the water gurgling. Robyn must, too, because her face suddenly lights up.

We rush down the rest of the way until we see the clear water coursing along its path, carrying leaves, twigs and the shadows of branches overhead.

I kneel by the river and scoop some of the water into my cupped hands. I splash them on my face just as Robyn did with her water earlier and feel the immediate relief.

Yet that relief is fleeting.

It's not enough.

I stand up, shrug off my backpack and take off my shirt.

"You're taking a bath?" Robyn asks.

The surprise in her voice is obvious.

I turn to her as I sit on a rock. "Why not?"

I take off my shoes and reach for the button of my khaki shorts.

"Wait," Robyn says. "You're taking off your shorts and your boxers, too?"

I grin as I slip my shorts off. "Sorry to disappoint you, but I'm leaving the boxers on."

I feel her gaze on my last piece of clothing just before she turns away with even redder cheeks.

I step into the water. The pebbles feel hard but cool against the weary soles of my feet.

I wade into the river until the water is above my waist. With each step, I feel the heat dissipate. Then I bend my knees until it pools around my neck. I swallow a gulp of air and go under for as long as I can.

When I can no longer hold my breath, I stand up. The cool water cascades down my skin and a refreshing wave washes over me as the air caresses it.

Now that's better.

I wipe my face and turn towards Robyn.

"Robyn, you should..."

I pause as I see her at the water's edge, completely naked. Her arms are crossed over her breasts, her hands cupping them to conceal her nipples. But everything else is exposed to my gaze, which I can't help but direct towards her.

"Skinny dipping, huh?" I say as my gaze falls between her legs. "And there you were complaining about me taking off my shorts."

"I wasn't complaining," Robyn says as she steps into the water. "And stop looking, will you?"

"Why? It's not like I haven't seen everything."

She frowns.

"Doesn't this feel like that time when I first saw you?" I ask.

She wades into the water. "I'd rather not remember that."

"I don't think I'll ever forget it."

She lets out a moan of contentment as she submerges herself in the water up to her shoulders. The sound goes straight to my crotch.

I frown. It seems not even this cool water can beat that kind of heat.

I swim towards her against the current.

"The water feels great, doesn't it?"

Robyn nods. "This is nostalgic, too."

I narrow my eyes at her. "You used to swim in rivers?"

She shrugs. "Lakes. But yeah, we used to go swimming when we went camping. In fact, I think I've been in more lakes than I've been in pools."

"Good for you. Pool water is like 90% urine."

She makes an expression of disgust. "And how can you be sure no one peed in this river?"

She scoops out a handful of water and lets it trickle through the gaps between her fingers.

"Animals don't pee in the water and there aren't any people for miles around here," I tell her.

She gets another handful and lifts it to her lips. "Well, it doesn't taste like pee."

I throw her a puzzled look. "You know what pee tastes like?"

"I don't..." She stops to roll her eyes, then splashes water on me.

I turn to my side so the water falls mostly on my shoulders.

"I take it back," Robyn says. "I don't like you after all."

"Really?" I move closer to her.

Her eyebrows crease. "What are you doing?"

"Finding out for sure whether you like me or not."

I lean forward and press my lips to hers. They remain still at first, then they push back against me.

I grin and pull away. "See, you *do* like me."

"I like you better when you're not talking."

She pulls my face close to hers for another kiss. I grab her by the buttocks and pull her close to me. My cock pushes against the damp cotton.

Suddenly, though, Robyn stops. Her hands drop from the sides of my face as she looks around.

"What's wrong?" I ask her.

"Do you hear that?" She moves away from me.

"Hear what?"

I don't hear anything at first, but after a few seconds, I do hear meowing.

"Poor cat," Robyn says, already halfway out the water. "It must be stuck up in a tree."

I let out a sigh. "Cats in trees. They always manage to spoil my fun."

"What was that?"

"Nothing."

Robyn dries herself and puts her clothes on. I wait for my erection to wilt before I get out of the water and do the same.

I follow her as she follows the sound. After a few minutes, we finally see the tabby cat up a tree branch.

Robyn clasps her hands together. "There you are."

"I didn't peg you for a cat lover," I tell her.

She ignores me and starts to climb.

"Whoa." I pull her arm. "What are you doing?"

"Rescuing a cat," she answers.

"Of course you are." I sigh. "Let me do it."

"Are you sure?"

I reach for the lowest branch. "This is kind of my forte?"

"Climbing trees?"

I don't answer. I simply hoist myself up on the lowest branch and then the next.

Of course this would be easier if I had a ladder, but I'm on my own on this one.

Finally, I get to the branch where the cat is. It immediately hisses at me.

"Now, this is nostalgic," I mutter to myself before turning to the cat.

It hisses louder. I glimpse the tips of its claws.

I roll my eyes and shout down at Robyn. "It's got a temper. Then again, they all do."

"It's just scared," she shouts back.

I shake my head as I look at the cat. "Why is it that you cats are so good at going up but so bad at coming down?"

"Just shake the branch," Robyn says. "I'll catch it."

I look down. "Are you sure?"

She nods.

I wait until she's in position, then start shaking the branch. Leaves cascade to the ground as the cat clings to the wood.

"Come on," I urge, shaking harder.

Finally, the cat slips. It hangs on the branch by its front paws. Another shake and it tumbles down right into Robyn's arms. She loses her balance for a moment but quickly regains it.

By the time I get back to the ground, she's cradling the cat like a baby and it's snuggling against her, purring with delight.

Of course the cat likes her.

Its ears spring up when it sees me. Then it jumps off Robyn's arms and runs off.

"Wait!" Robyn calls after it.

But it's gone.

"Yup. Go run off without a word of thanks," I say.

Robyn sighs and rubs her arms. "Do you think he'll be fine?"

"I'm sure of it," I tell her. "As long as he doesn't climb up another tree. Unfortunately, cats aren't very smart."

"Yes they are," she argues. "Oh well. I just hope it finds its way back home safely."

She walks back to the river and I follow her.

"Shall we continue?"

Yes, I'd very much like to continue.

She grabs her backpack.

Ah. She means continue hiking.

"I think I'm a little refreshed now," Robyn says.

"Me too." I put on my own backpack.

I would've felt better, though, if we hadn't been so rudely interrupted.

Stupid cat.

Well, hopefully, we'll have a chance to pick up where we left off later.

~

"This is your last chance," Robyn says.

We're lying beside each other, our backs flat on our sleeping bags and our eyes tilted towards the starry skies. Behind us, the fire crackles as it feeds on its pyre.

"If you don't guess this one, your MP3 player is as good as mine."

"Fine." I lift my beer bottle to my lips and take a sip. "Is it a zebra?"

"No," Robyn answers. "I already said it doesn't have stripes."

I frown. "I'm bad at Twenty Questions."

"Apparently," she says before taking a sip from her own bottle. "You have one question left, so this is really your last chance."

I set my bottle down and pause to think. "Is it a... hippo?"

"Nope." She shakes her head as she sits up. "And I've won. Your MP3 player is mine."

She claps her hands like a kid who's just won a prize at a birthday party.

Oh well. I would have given it to her anyway.

"What was the answer?" I ask her.

"A giraffe."

I feel confused. "You said it didn't have horns."

"Giraffes don't have horns," Robyn says as she reaches across me to get my MP3 player. "They're not bone, just cartilage."

I wrap my arms around her and pull her on top of me. "Smarty pants."

"Better than dumb pants," she says.

I stare into her deep brown eyes.

"Let me go," she says halfheartedly. "I'm blocking your view."

"On the contrary, my view just got way better."

I lift a hand to touch her cheek.

"And I need to get my MP3 player," she adds.

"Don't worry. It's yours." I stroke her cheek. "But there's something I need from you, too."

I lift my face to hers so that our lips can meet. This time, Robyn kisses me back at once and my heart drums. Heat rushes to my crotch.

I let my fingers get lost in her hair as I kiss her harder. Her red locks tumble like a curtain around us.

She cups my face and parts her lips. I push my tongue in even as I pull her body on top of mine. Her breasts weigh on my chest. My cock quivers excitedly against her thigh.

I want nothing more than to roll on top of her and to put something other than my tongue inside her. My body is burning hotter than the campfire and the anticipation is already making the tip of my cock melt.

Instead, I let my arms fall to my sides and my head against the pillow.

Robyn looks at me curiously. "Xander?"

"I'm just making sure you like the sex this time." I take her hand and press a kiss to her scarred palm. "So do what you like. I'm curious to know about it, too."

"Okay." She tucks strands of hair behind her ear. "Well, I didn't mean that, but yeah, I'll gladly take your offer."

She straddles my hips and rubs against my crotch. My cock pulses and I take a deep breath.

Maybe this wasn't the best idea.

Robyn seems genuinely pleased, though. Her lips curve into a grin and her eyes gleam with excitement... and mischief.

She grabs the hem of my shirt and pulls it off.

"You really like me shirtless, don't you?" I ask her.

Robyn doesn't answer. Her eyes are boring into skin and muscle. Her hand goes to the side of my neck.

"Is this tattoo a lightning bolt?" she asks.

I nod. "I thought you've seen it."

She shakes her head. "Is it because of your last name?"

"Yeah. It's older than the phoenix."

Her hand slides down my shoulder and my arm. The feather-light brushes of her fingertips send heat through my veins. Her touch on the inside of my elbow makes me suppress a laugh.

Robyn gives me a look of surprise. "That tickles?"

I nod. "But don't tell anyone."

She grins as her fingers walk down my arm all the way down to the wrist. The grin vanishes as she turns to my other arm.

"Where's this from?" She traces the scar on my right upper arm.

"You'll never guess."

Her eyes narrow. "Tell me."

"Or?"

She rubs against me again. "Or I'll stop and go to sleep."

I frown. "It's from rescuing a cat up a tree."

Her eyebrows shoot up. "No way."

"Yes way."

Robyn chuckles, then bends down to kiss the scar. The gesture tickles and arouses at the same time. I draw in a breath.

She plants a kiss in the middle of my chest before splaying her palms against my abdomen. The muscles quiver and tighten.

"How did you get to be so fit?" She runs her fingers over a spool of muscle.

"Same as everyone else," I answer hoarsely. "Exercise."

"Ah."

She moves lower and settles between my legs. Her lips press against my stiff cock through the layers of fabric and a gasp escapes me.

I seem to hear an amused chuckle just before she pulls the waistband of my shorts and my boxers down. My cock springs free before her eyes.

She stares at it like a child staring at a fish in an aquarium, then wraps her fingers around it. I inhale sharply and look away. My gaze pierces the skies above.

When the tip of her tongue grazes the tip of my cock, my eyes fall shut and my jaw clenches. When her lips wrap around it, my fingers curl around the fabric of the sleeping bag. My nails scrape the ground beneath.

Inch by inch, Robyn fits me inside her mouth and swallows.

"Fuck!" the obscenity escapes my lips as I lift my head.

My eyes open just as she starts to move her head back and forth. Our eyes meet and I swallow.

Fuck, indeed.

"Robyn..."

She seems to understand what I'm trying to say, because she lifts her head and pulls away. She wipes the saliva from the corners of her mouth and the sheer coating on her lips with the back of her hand.

She stands up and her pants and panties fall to the ground beside me. I catch the scent of her arousal.

She climbs back on top of me and claims my mouth as she straddles me anew. The tip of my cock brushes against her curls and I shiver.

Finally, she takes my cock and puts it inside her as I watch. My cock throbs in its wet, velvety sheath. My hips, which suddenly take on a mind of their own, rise up to thrust deep inside her.

Robyn lets out a soft moan, places her hands on my shoulders, and starts moving her own hips to meet mine. Her hair tickles my cheeks. I glimpse her breasts past the neckline of her shirt.

I pull the shirt off her and sit up to take a firm breast in my mouth. My tongue swirls around her nipple and she shivers.

I do the same to the other and she cries out before pushing me back down. Her breasts bounce as she continues to move her hips. Her eyes fall shut and her hair dangles past her shoulders as she throws her head back.

I cup the cheeks of her backside, firmly rounded like her breasts. I give them a tight squeeze as I bury my teeth into my lower lip.

I can tell from the look on her face that she's on the brink of losing control.

And so am I.

When she stops to rest and catch her breath, I clutch her shoulders and push her down on her sleeping bag. I grab her hips and begin pounding into her. Her back arches. Her mouth opens and stays that way to let out one cry after another.

I fold her nearly in half and push even deeper inside her.

I can feel the tumultuous heat swirling inside me, aching to break free.

I kiss her through the gap between her trembling legs as I let go. My cock jerks as I empty myself inside her. Her nails dig into my back as she milks me of every drop.

When I'm finally spent, I collapse on top of Robyn. Her gasps for air mingle with mine. Her fingers caress the hair on my nape.

I lift my head and gaze into her eyes. They glisten like the stars behind me. I see myself in them and my chest tightens.

"How do you feel?" I ask her softly.

Robyn's lips curve into a grin. "Amazing."

Chapter Eleven

Robyn

"I don't feel so good," I tell Xander as I blow my nose on a piece of tissue.

Already, I've been to the bathroom twice to throw up. My chest feels crushed, as if an elephant just walked all over it. My throat feels like it's been scratched by an eagle's claws. My eyes and nose are leaking, my head's splitting in two, and oh, my stomach is still churning even though I'm pretty sure it's already empty.

The last pile I threw up looked like bananas, which were the last thing I ate. I can still remember the slightly sour, slightly bitter taste even though the minty toothpaste has already scrubbed it off my tongue.

Yes, I feel rotten.

Xander places a hand on my sweat-drenched forehead. "You don't seem to have a fever, so it's not the flu."

"It's mostly my stomach, I think." I rub my temples. "And my head."

He shrugs. "Well, maybe it's just a hangover."

"From just two bottles?" I pout as I rest my head against the pillow. "Xander, don't make me sound like a wimp."

"You're not a wimp," he assures me. "You were dehydrated yesterday. And then the cold air from last night and the climb down might have upset your stomach."

My stomach gurgles in affirmation.

"Whatever." I exhale. "I'm just tired. Really tired."

"Rest." Xander squeezes my hand. "It's only Aaron and me left and there's not much to do. We'll make our own food."

I squeeze his hand back. "Sorry."

Xander frowns. "You're not regretting sleeping with me again, are you?"

"No," I tell him. "I enjoyed every moment of our camping trip, including that part."

It's true. Sex last night was amazing, especially since Xander allowed me to take control for a while, which never even crossed Howie's mind. And while yesterday's camping trip wasn't the same as when I used to go camping with Mom, Dad and Wesley, it was close. The spirit of adventure was there. The communion with nature was there. The excitement. The tranquility. The stars. The s'mores.

At the memory of marshmallows toasting over the fire and getting just a little crisp and charred on the outside and soft and gooey on the inside, my mouth waters.

I'm not exactly hungry after all that throwing up, but I wish I had one right now.

"What is it?" Xander asks.

"Nothing." I swallow. "I just thought a s'more would be nice."

His eyes grow wide. "A s'more?"

I don't answer.

"Well, I'm glad to hear that you had fun." Xander pulls the blanket up to my chin. "Now, rest."

I pull the blanket higher up to my nose. Xander's scent drifts into my nostrils along with the aroma of...

"Coffee?" I sniff.

"I think I spilled some before." Xander scratches his head. "Though I thought I washed it out. I can get you another blanket if you want."

"It's fine," I assure him. "It still smells nice."

I take another sniff, then toss the blanket aside.

Xander's eyebrows furrow. "It smells nice but you don't like it?"

"I'm not cold. In fact, I feel very warm."

Even though I'm wearing a thin shirt and the air conditioning is on, I still feel like I'm in a sauna.

"Okay." Xander checks the thermostat on the wall. "Want me to lower the temp?"

"Yes, please." I rest my hands on my stomach, which has managed to calm down a little. "62 would be nice."

"62?" Xander turns to me with wide eyes. "What are you? A stick of butter? If it's too cold, you might get sicker."

"But I feel warm," I argue.

He sighs and turns the knob. "Just promise me you won't freeze."

I turn on my side so that my back is against him and yawn. "If I freeze, you can just warm me up again."

He says nothing, but I can tell he's grinning.

"Sorry. I think I'll sleep now," I tell him.

"You do that. Get your strength back. And if you need anything, just let me know."

"You sound like my mother," I mumble.

Still, I have to admit it feels good to have someone taking care of me.

"I'll check on you later."

His footsteps fade. Moments later, the door opens and closes.

I turn on my other side and tuck a pillow beneath my leg.

Xander's right. I have to get my strength back. If I don't, I won't be able to leave.

Strange, though. Things were worse the whole time I was with Howie, and yet I never felt unwell. In pain, yes, but not unwell. In fact, I don't remember being this sick since that time I ate spoiled food from the cafeteria when I was in sixth grade.

I let out a sigh and turn on my back.

Oh well. I'll just have to get better.

~

"Are you sure you're feeling better?" Xander asks me as we step inside the house.

"If you're asking if I'm going to throw up and ruin Caitlin's precious rugs or furniture, I won't," I promise him.

He closes the door behind him. "That's not what I was asking, but okay. I'm glad you're feeling better."

He takes my hand and leads me down the hall. The wooden floor gleams beneath my feet. Rustic chandeliers hang above me like dangling works of art, impressive even when turned off.

At the end of the hall, we go up the spiral staircase. I grab one of the railings.

"These came out pretty good," I remark as I run my fingers over the polished wood.

"They did," Xander agrees. "Mike may be young and his mouth may run away with him sometimes, but he's good with his hands."

I glance at him. "Hey. I helped, too."

He tugs at my arm. "Come on."

We reach the second floor and he leads me down another hall then up another spiral staircase, narrower than the first.

"Where are we going?" I ask him.

He doesn't answer. He just takes me to a large door at the top of the staircase.

"Ready?" He grabs the doorknob.

I nod.

He turns it and pushes the door open. I step into the room with wide eyes.

There are no chandeliers here, just lamps on a large, round table in the middle of the room. Heavy shelves stocked with books line the walls. A modern fireplace occupies a corner with matching rocking chairs in front of it. A painted family portrait stands watch on the mantel.

I hold back a gasp as I run my fingers over the table.

I've seen many of the other rooms in the house and I know they're all beautiful, but this room—this is just breathtaking.

And then my gaze falls on the stained glass window at the end of the room. The fragments of colored glass split the sunlight into a glittering rainbow that paints the floor. My heart stops.

I take that back. This room isn't just breathtaking. It's... magical.

"Well? What do you think?" Xander asks.

I turn to him. "As much as I hate to admit it, Caitlin has a bit of talent."

Xander nods.

I turn back to the window. "But Joel is definitely more talented. That window is just..."

I raise my hands and let them fall on my sides.

"I'm at a loss for words."

"Joel thought you'd be happy to see it."

I step closer to the window and lift my arm to touch the glass. I smile as the colors dance on my skin.

"I am," I admit before turning around. "Thank him for me, will you?"

"You can thank him yourself," Xander says.

I nod. "Right. You can give me his number. I'll thank him when I get a phone."

"That's not what I meant." He steps closer to me. "Robyn, I've been thinking..."

"About?"

"You don't have to leave," he says. "You can continue working for me. You know I could use your skills."

I fall silent, shocked by the unexpected offer. That option did already cross my mind, but I dismissed it. I don't want to get more attached to Xander and the guys than I already am. Sooner or later, Howie will find me and I'll have to leave. I don't want to get any of them into trouble. I can't let anyone else pay for my mistakes.

I walk over to the nearest bookshelf and run my fingers over the spines of a few books. "You know I can't stay, Xander."

"Why not?"

I turn to face him. "Because I can't! We talked about this, Xander. When I first came here, you told me I'd only work for you until the project was over."

"That was the initial arrangement," he agrees. "But do you really think nothing has changed since then?"

I slap my forehead. "I knew I shouldn't have slept with you."

He grabs my hand. "This isn't about that. We both know you have nowhere else to go."

"I'll find a place."

"I'm offering you a place. A safe place."

I pull my hand away and shake my head. "Xander, I don't need your protection."

"Are you saying it's okay for you to go back where you came from? To relive your nightmares?"

A lump forms in my throat.

"Robyn, you can't run away forever."

"Yes, I can," I tell him. "I can do what I want with my life because it's mine."

He reaches for my hand again. "Let me help you."

I move away. "Why should I? Why do you want to help me so badly anyway?"

"Because I don't want you to get hurt again," Xander answers. "When we first met, I promised no harm would come to you."

"No harm has come to me here."

"I meant ever."

I shake my head. "That's not up to you, Xander."

He pauses and pain flickers in his eyes. My chest tightens.

"Believe me, I know," he goes on. "But I'll be damned if I don't do anything."

I draw a deep breath. "Well, thanks for the offer, but my answer is no. I'm leaving when you are, and you can't..."

I stop as my stomach suddenly flips again.

Shit. I got upset, so now my stomach got upset too.

"Robyn?"

As it turns again, I feel its contents rise to my chest. I clasp a hand over my mouth and run out of the house as fast as I can. As soon as I'm outside, my knees give way and I sink to the ground, leaning on my arms as I throw up.

When I'm done, I wipe my mouth with the back of my hand and lie down on the ground. I close my eyes as my head begins to spin.

What the hell is wrong with me?

Chapter Twelve

Xander

"Maybe we should bring you to a hospital," I suggest as I hand Robyn a glass of water.

She shakes her head before taking a sip.

"No. No hospitals."

The adamant refusal makes me wonder, but I don't ask. "Okay."

She hands me back the glass and I set it down on the table.

"What about a doctor, then? I know one. Maybe we can..."

"I'll be fine," Robyn cuts me off. "It's just... stress."

She means she was upset by our conversation earlier, which was obvious anyway.

But why? I was only trying to help her. I knew she'd be reluctant to accept my offer, but I didn't think she'd refuse so violently. What did she have to lose? She doesn't have a family to run to, a place to go to. She has no money other than what I've given her, which is bound to run out soon.

Why won't Robyn take my offer? Pride? No. I have a feeling it's something more, but she won't tell me. After all this time and after all that's happened between us, she still doesn't trust me.

"I'll be fine, okay?" She turns her back to me. "Just... leave me alone."

I nod. "I'll be right outside."

I mean that literally. I leave the room and close the door but stand right outside it. After a while, I hear her sobbing.

My eyebrows perk up. She's that upset?

I glance at the door. A part of me wants to rush back inside so I can wrap my arms around her like I did when she had that nightmare. Instead, I go outside the trailer with a clenched jaw.

Whatever it is Robyn's going through right now, it's real and she has to deal with it alone. She's the only one who can.

Outside the trailer, I draw a deep breath and take my phone out of my pocket.

Robyn said she didn't want a doctor's help, but I, for one, would like to know what's going on. Maybe she is just upset, but I want to be sure it's nothing serious.

I pull out an old friend's number and make the call.

"Hello." I hear Beth's voice on the other end of the line.

"Beth, how are you? It's me, Xander."

There's a pause. "Xander? Alexander Bolt?"

"Same."

She gasps. "I haven't heard from you in…"

"Six years," I finish the sentence for her. "You haven't changed your number."

"I waste too much time changing masks and gloves. Why change something I don't have to?"

I grin. Old Beth. She's just as I remember her.

"Hey. I just wanted to ask you something."

"And here I thought you called just to wish me a happy birthday."

My eyebrows furrow. "It's your birthday?"

"No. I'm just messing with you. What's the favor?"

"Listen, I know you work mostly with unconscious people…"

"I am a surgeon, after all."

"But I have a medical question regarding an adult."

"I'm guessing you're not talking about yourself."

"No," I answer.

"A girlfriend?" Beth asks.

"A friend," I correct.

"Ah."

"She's been throwing up lately and she says her stomach hurts and her head hurts."

"Did she eat something?"

"She and I have been eating the same things and I'm perfectly fine."

"Maybe the stomach flu? In which case you just need to make sure she doesn't get dehydrated. It will pass."

I nod. "That's what I thought. I just wanted a second opinion."

"Or she could be pregnant."

The suggestion makes me pause. I glance back at the trailer.

"Say that again?"

"Upset stomach. Dizziness. Fatigue. They're all symptoms of pregnancy."

And so is having a sensitive sense of smell, I think as I recall her catching the scent of coffee on my blanket.

Fuck.

"When was the last time your friend had her period?" Beth asks.

I shrug. "I don't know."

But I do know that she hasn't had it since she got here.

Fuck.

"Xander?"

"Thanks for taking my call, Beth," I tell her. "I have to go now."

"No worries. And Xander?"

I put my phone back to my ear. "Yes?"

"Do the right thing."

She hangs up and I put my phone back in my pocket. I sit on a nearby stool and run my hands through my head in frustration.

Robyn's pregnant?

Now that I think of it, it's possible. It's not my child, of course. There simply hasn't been enough time.

But as much as I loathe to admit it, I know I'm not the only one who's had sex with her.

She didn't have any clothes on when I first saw her, just cuts and bruises. She said she's sworn off men, but she doesn't seem to be a virgin.

Nope. She's had sex with other men, probably recently, so of course there's a chance she's pregnant.

I think of the dizzy spells and the vomiting. And the sensitive nose and the craving for s'mores. And the sobbing.

Now I know why she's upset.

I shake my head. No. I'm not yet sure if she's pregnant.

But I know how to find out.

~

"What's this?" Robyn asks as I hand her the brown paper bag from the pocket of my sweater.

I don't answer. I just let her open it.

Her eyes grow wide.

"A preg—?"

"It's best to consider all the possibilities," I cut her off. "And be prepared for all the outcomes."

Robyn's face grows pale. For a moment, she says nothing as she stares at the pregnancy test on her lap. Then she nods.

"Okay."

I place my hand on her shoulder. "Whatever happens, I'm here for you."

She doesn't answer.

I squeeze her shoulder and walk out the door. Again, I stand right outside it with my ears perked up.

For a while, I hear nothing. Robyn must still be on the bed, still in shock at the idea I've just put forward. Of course she would be. Just as I never thought of the possibility until Beth mentioned it, she hasn't considered it before either.

After a few minutes, I hear footsteps on the floor. I hear another door open and close.

The bathroom.

I hold my breath and try to still my pounding heart as I wait for the door to open again.

Instead, I hear a wail.

Chapter Thirteen

Robyn

My mouth gapes open as I hold the pregnancy test with my shaking hands. The two red lines blur as tears fill my eyes.

No.

I can't be pregnant. I can't.

I'm on the run. I don't have a family or a home or a job. I don't know the first thing about babies.

But none of those are valid arguments, just fears.

On the other hand, I have facts to confirm my pregnancy.

I've had unprotected sex, with Howie and then with Xander. I risked it because when I had my childhood accident, a splinter hit one of my ovaries and the doctor told my mother I might have a hard time conceiving. She never said it was impossible, though.

I haven't had my period in... well, nearly two months now, though I thought it was just because of all the stress I was going through. Plus I was never regular, a fact I also attributed to my accident.

Lately, I've been having headaches and I've been throwing up, which are both widely known indications of pregnancy. Then, of course, there's the proof in my hands.

Two red lines.

Well, it could be wrong, but I don't think so.

I am pregnant.

I clamp my hand over my gaping mouth as the tears trickle down my cheeks.

Now what?

It's only been a little over a week since Xander and I first had sex, so I know the baby isn't his. I know exactly who it belongs to.

Howie.

The realization stabs my chest like a knife.

I don't want to have Howie's baby. He's a monster. He put me through hell.

What then? Do I get rid of this baby?

My hand falls to my belly. I can't feel any movement yet, but I can tell there's something inside.

No. Someone.

What do I do?

"Robyn?" Xander calls from beyond the door. "Can I come in?"

I don't answer at once. I'm not sure if I want to see him or talk to him.

Then again, I'm already in the worst situation there is. He can't possibly upset me more.

Besides, in spite of all I've been through, I've never felt more alone. And for the first time, it scares me.

I open the door and Xander comes in.

"Robyn."

At once, he takes me in his arms. The pregnancy test clatters to the floor.

As before, I let my tears loose against the front of his shirt. I tremble against his chest.

He leads me out of the bathroom towards the bed. I drop on its edge and he sits beside me. One of his arms wraps tightly around me. His other hand strokes my hair as he tucks my head beneath his chin.

I cry until my tears have all ran out. Then I pull away.

Xander hands me a box of tissues. I pull one out and blow my nose. Then I grab another.

"Sorry," I mumble as I wipe my tears.

Xander shakes his head. "You don't have to apologize for anything. I told you I'm here for you."

I stare at the crumpled tissue in my hands. "I don't know what to do."

"Most people in your situation don't." He places his hand over mine. "You just have to figure it out."

I lift my head to meet his gaze.

He squeezes my hand. "What do you want to do, Robyn?"

I place a hand over my belly. "I... I don't think I can get rid of the baby. And I'm not sure I want to. Whoever his or her father may be, this baby is a different person. And he or she is innocent."

Xander nods. "No one is asking you to kill your own baby."

"But can I really keep it?" I look into his eyes once more as fresh tears sting mine. "I have nothing."

"You have me," Xander tells me as he puts his other hand over mine.

I shake my head. "This isn't your problem, Xander. I can't..."

"I want to help you, Robyn," he interrupts me. "And whether you like it or not, you need my help. You and your baby need my help."

I purse my lips.

Xander's right. I didn't want his help before, and before I could have done without it, somehow. But now, the situation has changed. It's not just my life that's in danger here. It's the baby's. My baby's. If I want to protect my baby from Howie, to make sure he or she lives a good life or at least has a chance at it, I need Xander's help.

"What exactly are you offering?" I ask him.

"I'll take care of you and your baby," Xander answers.

"Even if the baby isn't yours?"

"It's yours," he says. "That's enough reason for me to take care of it."

I look down at my stomach.

Again, Xander's right. This baby may be Howie's, but it's also mine.

As I stroke my belly, a fierce protectiveness wells inside my chest and grips my heart.

No. This baby is just mine, all mine.

I'll do whatever it takes to protect it, even if that means taking advantage of other people's kindness.

I squeeze Xander's hand. "Well, if you're going to help me, I guess I should let you know what you're getting into."

He exhales. "Finally."

I move back so I can lean on the wall. "Where do I begin?"

"At the beginning," Xander suggests.

"After my parents died, I... kind of got lost," I start. "I fell in with the wrong crowd. They drank. They smoked. And not just cigarettes."

"So those were the parties you were talking about."

I nod. "Howie was part of that crowd."

"Howie?" Xander throws me a puzzled look.

"Howard Mitchell," I explain. "He became my boyfriend."

Xander falls silent. His jaw visibly clenches.

He knows the hard part is coming.

I draw a deep breath, then clasp my hands together. "Howie was nice at first. But then he started wanting more and more from me. And when he got tired of asking, he just took."

Xander's hands roll into fists.

I stroke one of my thumbs with the other. "I wanted to leave him but I couldn't. I was so scared and I had no one to help me."

"You didn't think of going to the cops?" Xander asks.

I shake my head. "Howie was with a bunch of people. They all hated cops. Besides, I wasn't sure the cops weren't going to arrest me, too. I didn't want to go to jail."

"I understand."

"Well, I didn't want to go to jail at first, but as things got worse, I started to think jail wouldn't be so bad. I even started to think death might not be so bad."

Xander inhales sharply.

"Then one day, Howie just disappeared. They said he was killed in some alley. I didn't bother with the details. I was finally free. At least, I thought I was."

I fold my legs beneath me.

"For years, my life was close to normal. I wasn't happy, exactly, but I was okay. At least I had a life. And then out of the blue, Howie came back."

"Came back?"

"As it turns out, he didn't die. He just got hurt really bad. When he finally recovered, he began searching for me, and he finally found me." I grip my pants. "He caused a scene at work, hurt some people, too. Then he took me and plunged me back into hell."

"Asshole," Xander mutters under his breath.

"As you know, I escaped," I continue. "And I ended up in one of your trucks and then here. You know the rest."

Xander says nothing. He just stands up and touches his chin. His eyebrows furrow in contemplation.

I move back to the edge of the bed. "What a tragic backstory, huh?"

"It does pose a problem," he says.

I frown. "If it's too much for you, you don't have to..."

"We'll have to get married," Xander blurts out as he turns to face me.

My eyebrows go up. "Excuse me?"

"We'll get married," Xander explains. "We'll say the baby is mine. That way, Howie will stop trying to take you back."

I blink. "Are you sure? You don't have to go that far."

"I do. Even now, Howie is looking for you. He wants you back. But if you belong to someone else, he can't have you."

I let out a sigh. "I don't think Howie will give up that easily."

"But he'll have to." Xander grasps my chin. "Because I won't let him have you."

The words, spoken with utmost sincerity, make my breath catch and my heart stop. It takes me a while to answer.

"You're... serious?"

Xander nods as he grabs my hand. "I've never been more serious."

"But what if he tries to hurt you?"

"Let him," he says through gritted teeth.

Rage simmers in his eyes.

"I promise I'll keep you and your baby safe," he continues.

And I believe him.

"And you don't mind getting married to someone who doesn't love you?" I ask him.

"I won't if you won't," he tells me with a softer expression.

Right. I don't love him and he doesn't love me. We're just getting married to protect the baby from Howie.

"At least we like each other," Xander adds. "Besides, it doesn't have to be permanent. We'll find a way to make Howie pay for the things he did to you, and once he's rotting in jail, we can get a divorce."

A divorce?

Of course. Xander doesn't want to be married to me for real or for good. He doesn't seem like the marrying kind, and even if he was, he deserves someone better than me.

"I guess that makes sense," I say.

"Then it's all settled." Xander stands up and clasps his hands together. "We'll get married as soon as possible."

I still can't believe it. Just a few minutes ago, I found out I was pregnant. And now I'm getting married?

Suddenly, something occurs to me.

"What about your family?" I ask Xander. "Won't they be surprised?"

He grins and offers me his hand. "Why don't we go meet them and find out?"

~

The tires of the Expedition come to a stop in front of a three-story house built from logs and sheets of glass. A short bridge leads up to the massive front door where a pair of sculpted wolves stand guard. Flower beds with rows of yellow and pink blooms lie beneath the large windows. Three chimneys stick out of the roof.

I swallow the lump in my throat. "This is your home?"

"Technically, this house belongs to my aunt and uncle," Xander explains as he turns off the engine. "But yes, it's where I live."

Holy shit. This house is practically a mansion.

Then again, I should have expected something like this. I knew Xander had a lot of money. He owns a company, after all. And like he explained, the company used to belong to his uncle, so he must be rich, too. And it stands to reason that people who own a construction company would have good taste in houses.

"Why don't you have your own house?" I ask as I get out of the car.

"Still working on it," Xander answers.

Okay.

"Come on." He offers me his hand.

I draw a deep breath and take it. "Are you sure about this?"

"I thought we already talked this through."

"Yes, we did," I say. "But you didn't mention that your aunt and uncle were billionaires."

"Don't worry." Xander squeezes my hand. "They're not rich snobs. They're the nicest people I know, in fact."

I sigh. "Of course they're nice to you. You're their nephew."

"And you are going to be their niece," he tells me. "Or their niece-in-law or whatever it's called."

That there is the problem.

I run my hands through my hair. "Maybe I should have worn make-up and a dress."

All of a sudden, my green long-sleeved blouse and faded denim skirt seem inadequate. I pinch my cheeks just to make sure they're not too pale and run my fingertips just below my eyes to check that I don't have any bulging eye bags.

"You look great," Xander assures me as he tucks a loose strand of my hair behind my ear. "They'll love you."

I exhale.

Breathe, Robyn. Just breathe.

We walk the rest of the way in silence, across the bridge over the koi pond. When we reach the front door, Xander slips in his key and it opens to a spacious room. Sunlight floods in through the glass and bathes the elegant furniture.

"Geoffrey? Linda?" Xander calls. "I have someone I want you to meet."

After a few seconds, a man with thin grey hair and round, silver-rimmed eyeglasses descends the stairs. A woman with slightly darker hair twisted in a braid beneath a pink wide-brimmed hat and the exact same pair of glasses emerges from the end of a hall. From behind them, her eyes meet mine and she lifts both gloved hands to her mouth to conceal a gasp.

My heart pounds. This is it.

"Geoffrey, Linda," Xander says as he grips my hand tight in his. "I want you to meet my fiancée, Robyn."

Chapter Fourteen

Xander

"I knew you'd find the right woman," Linda tells me as she sprays a mist of water on one of her orchid plants.

I sit on a bench not far from her, right next to the table with her other spray bottles, a watering can and a pair of pruning shears. Rays of sunlight rain down on my face through the glass panels of the greenhouse.

"Did you now?" I ask her as I pick up the shears. "Because you seemed worried on my thirtieth birthday that I was going to be alone for the rest of my life."

"I was simply trying to give you a hint that I wanted you to get married," she says. "And look at you. You finally got it."

I frown.

I knew she wanted me to settle down, but I didn't know she wanted me to get married that badly.

I sit back and cross one leg over the other. "I take it you like her."

"She looks decent." Linda moves to the next orchid and pushes her glasses up and out of the way to take a closer look at its buds. "I remember that woman you brought home for my birthday once. She barely had anything on."

I don't really remember that. What I do remember is how Robyn looked when I first met her, and I suppress a grin as I wonder how shocked Linda would be if she found out.

"Besides, she complimented my flowers," Linda adds as she lets her glasses fall back on her nose.

I put the shears back on the table. "Anyone with eyes would."

"Not Carol. She hates the fact that my flowers always turn out better than hers even though she buys her stuff from the same place I do and she does the same things I do."

"Well, we both know Carol isn't nice," I point out. "So what she says or doesn't say doesn't count."

Linda pushes her glasses up her nose. "True. Oh, and Robyn didn't ask if the golden candlesticks were made of real gold. I take that as a good sign that she's not after money."

"She isn't," I assure her as I get off the bench.

"Is she from a rich family?"

"No," I answer. "She has no family."

"Oh."

Linda falls silent.

I stand beside her. "Is that a problem?"

She looks at me and shakes her head. "Why would it be? You love her, don't you? That's why you're so eager to marry her? And not because you feel sorry for her or you're trying to save her or for any other reason?"

This time, I'm the one who's silent.

Linda knows me so well. Of course she does. She's been like a mother to me.

She touches my cheek. "You're old enough, Xander. And you're wise. I trust you."

I place my hand over hers. "I'm doing the right thing."

She lets out a breath. "That's what I thought."

She pats my cheek.

"Well, you don't owe me any explanations. You know I support you and so does Geoffrey. If you're happy, we're happy."

I smile. "Thank you."

"However..." Linda lifts a finger. "There is someone who might need a little prodding."

I nod. I know very well who she's talking about.

"Jillian."

~

"You have a step-cousin?" Robyn turns away from the bedroom window to look at me with wide eyes.

I nod. "Jillian. My aunt and uncle adopted her when she was still a child. She's a year younger than I am, but she's quite bossy."

"Where is she?"

"She has a family of her own now—a husband and two kids. Two smart and rather unruly boys."

Robyn touches her chin. Her eyebrows furrow.

"What?" I ask her.

She taps her chin. "Does your cousin have brown hair, just a bit darker than yours?"

"Yes. Why?"

"I think I saw a picture of her and her sons on your computer... I thought she was your wife."

"My wife?" I give her a look of surprise. "What made you think I was married?"

She pouts. "Well, you did say you had a past, and it seems important people were involved, so I thought..."

"That I was married and that they left me because of something I did?"

Robyn shrugs.

I sigh. "Well, I admire your active imagination and I'm sorry to disappoint you, but Jillian is my cousin. She's married to a brilliant but constantly busy lawyer named Matt, who has a bit of money of his own. And like

I said, she has two kids—two boys named Maverick and Austin."

"They're about four and six, right?" Robyn asks.

"Are they?" I scratch my head. "A little older now."

"I see."

"And more mischievous, no doubt. Oh, and by the way, Jillian used to be a TV actress."

"She was?" Robyn's eyes grow wide.

I nod. "It was just for a few years and just some bit roles on a few not-so-well-known TV shows, but yeah. Unfortunately, that means she can tell when someone is acting."

"Oh." Robyn sits on a wingback chair. "That does pose a problem."

"Mm-hmm."

"Does she already know we're getting married?"

"Linda told her earlier. She's coming tomorrow."

Robyn's eyebrows bunch up. "So soon?"

"She can't wait to meet you."

She sighs. "Then I guess we've only got a few hours to get our facts straight."

"Don't worry." I occupy the chair across her. "We just have to come up with a believable story and stick to it."

"Okay."

"And one more thing." I take a gold band with a heart-shaped emerald out of my pocket and place it on my palm. "Linda gave this to me. She wants you to wear it."

Robyn stares at it, then shakes her head. "I can't possibly..."

I take her hand and put the ring on her palm. "It will help convince Jillian our engagement is real."

She lets out another sigh. "Fine."

Slowly, she slips the ring onto her finger.

"It has an emerald because even then, Linda loved plants," I explain. "Geoffrey is probably the only thing she loves more."

She holds the ring up to the light. "It's beautiful."

"And it seems to fit," I observe.

Robyn nods. "I guess."

I sit back and tap my fingers on the arm of the chair. "Now, all we need is a story."

~

"So, the two of you met through a common client?" Jillian asks with creased eyebrows as she sets down her cup of coffee.

"Exactly," I answer. "I was a building a house for him and she was crunching numbers for him."

"He wanted me to see the house to ask whether I thought it was worth the money he spent," Robyn continues. "And I bumped into Xander."

"Literally," I add. "I was carrying some tools and she was carrying some papers and we bumped into each other."

"Oh." Jillian's trimmed eyebrows crease even more. "And neither of you got hurt?"

"Thank goodness, no," Robyn answers before I can. "But my heart did skip a beat."

"I'm sure it did." Jillian picks up her cup. "When was this, again?"

"A year ago," I answer.

She narrows her eyes at me. "And you never told me about it."

"No."

"You were going out for a year and you didn't tell me."

"It was just an experiment," Robyn says.

Jillian's eyebrows arch. "An experiment?"

"We said we'd go out for a year, you know, just to try it out and have fun. I mean, we both weren't looking for anything serious. If it wasn't working after a year, we'd just walk away."

"But it did work," I say as I reach for Robyn's hand and look into her eyes. I just couldn't walk away from her."

"He proposed and I couldn't think of a reason to say no," Robyn adds.

"Really?" Jillian picks up her cup and sits back.

"Really," I tell her.

She takes a sip. "And this happened just a few days ago?"

"Yes."

"And you want to get married in a week?"

"Yes." I squeeze Robyn's hand. "Why wait when we enjoy each other's company so much?"

"And you think that's enough reason to get married?" Jillian's eyebrows arch again. "Just because you enjoy each other's company?"

Robyn shrugs. "Why not?"

Jillian sets down her cup. "And is this company just in bed or...?"

"Jillian," I scold her.

"What?" Her shoulders rise. "I just want to know that you're not just marrying her because the sex is good."

"Well, I won't say the sex isn't good."

That, at least, isn't a lie.

"But that's not the only reason."

Jillian looks at Robyn. "You're not pregnant, are you?"

"No," Robyn answers quickly. "Of course not."

Jillian turns to me.

"She's not pregnant," I lie.

She nods. "Okay."

I suppress a sigh of relief.

"Fine. So you're in love and you're getting married next week?"

"Yes," Robyn and I answer at the same time.

She grins. "What a nice story."

"It's true, though," I tell her.

"Of course it is." She stands up and glances at Robyn. "By the way, I see you have Mom's ring. When did she give it to you?"

"Yesterday," Robyn answers.

Jillian takes her hand and looks at the ring. "I wore it, too, before I got married. It brought me luck. I hope it will give you good luck, too."

Robyn smiles. "I hope so."

"Now, if you'll excuse me, I have to check on my boys."

Jillian leaves the room. As soon as she does, Robyn beats me to a sigh of relief.

"Do you think she believed us?" she asks.

"I think so," I answer as I let go of her hand. "And I think she likes you."

"Oh, by the way," Jillian says as she returns to the living room.

I quickly grab Robyn's hand. "Yes?"

"I'll be taking care of most of the wedding planning and I have a few errands to run tomorrow." She turns to Robyn. "Do you think you can watch the boys for me?"

Robyn nods. "Sure."

"Sweet." Jillian grins and leaves again.

Once she's out of sight, I lean over Robyn and whisper in her ear. "I take it back. I don't think she likes you."

"Oh, come on." She nudges my shoulder. "It's just watching two adorable boys. How hard can it be?"

Chapter Fifteen

Robyn

Not that hard, I conclude as I carefully pry the tablet from beneath a sleeping Maverick's fingers.

One of them twitches and I hold my breath, but other than that he doesn't move. His eyelids, fringed with thick lashes, remain shut. His chest rises and falls steadily with his breathing.

I let out a sigh of relief as I put the gadget on the coffee table. I glance over at Austin, who's also asleep on the bean bag, and my lips curve into a smile.

Yes, they were unruly, as most boys are. Yes, they got their heads drenched in sweat while running in the yard and the whole counter dirty while baking cookies. Yes, they fought over whose cookies turned out better and started punching each other. Yes, they got me wet while I was giving them baths. Yes, they beat me at every video game. And yes, they made me watch gross videos of people with too much time eating things they shouldn't. It's a miracle I didn't get sick.

My throat hurts from shouting. My eyes hurt from constantly following their every move. My feet hurt from walking. I'm so tired.

Still, I had fun. The sweet smiles they gave me every now and then were enough to turn my frowns upside down and replenish my patience. Each time their rowdy laughter charged the air, I felt a fresh boost of energy. And when they hugged me with their sweaty arms and sticky hands, my heart couldn't help but melt.

I put away the video games and controllers before sitting on the couch. I grab the Captain Underpants book and manage to read a few pages before a yawn wrenches my mouth open.

I guess I should take a nap as well.

Just as I'm about to close my eyes, though, I hear the clacking of heels coming down the stairs. I turn my head towards the doorway just as Jillian appears in her navy blue frilled blouse and white pants. Her red-rimmed sunglasses sit on the top of her head.

I hold a finger to my lips.

"Are they asleep?" she whispers as she tiptoes in.

I let Jillian see the answer for herself and watch as her almond-shaped ebony eyes grow wide.

She stands in the middle of the room and starts counting on her fingers. "Asleep. Clean. No scratches. No bruises." She sniffs. "And I don't smell any pee."

She turns to me with arms crossed over her chest.

"Robyn, I'm impressed."

I smile. That wasn't exactly my goal, but now that she's said it I can't help but feel proud of myself. Whatever remaining tiredness I feel evaporates.

"They're handfuls, I'll admit," I tell her as I stand up and walk to her side. "But they're not that bad. They're just... boys."

"I know." Jillian sighs. "It's just that sometimes when they pee all over your bathroom or get snot all over your fresh satin sheets, you can't help but wish they were girls."

I grin. I can imagine.

"But hey." She ushers me up the stairs. "At least when they're older I won't have to wash their bloody underwear or hear them complain about having small breasts or running out of lipstick."

My eyebrows arch as my gaze inadvertently goes to her chest. She looks fairly well endowed. It's hard to imagine they used to be small.

Unless she had underwent breast augmentation, which a lot of TV stars do.

"Oh, these?" She pats her breasts as she notices my stare.

I look away and blush.

"It's all about the bra," she whispers in my ear. "I can tell you where you can get a great one."

She glances at my chest.

"Although you don't really need it."

I look down at my breasts. Indeed, I've noticed they've grown lately, so much so that I do need a new bra.

I smile at Jillian. "I'd love to know where you got them. The bras I mean."

She gives a light chuckle and pats my shoulder. "Girl, I sure am glad you passed the test. You have no idea how desperate I've been to hang out with someone who doesn't have testosterone."

My eyes grow wide. "Test?"

"Yup." Jillian gives me a thumbs-up sign as we reach the living room. "You passed the test."

I blink.

So Xander was right. Jillian was testing me.

"Sorry." She sits on the couch. "I just had to. After what Xander's last girlfriend did and all that Xander's been through, I just don't want him to get hurt."

I'm tempted to ask about what Xander's last girlfriend did, but I resist. As his fiancée, I'm supposed to know.

I just passed the test. I don't want to blow it.

More importantly, Jillian said she doesn't want Xander to get hurt. It sounds like a warning not to be taken lightly.

I swallow the lump in my throat as I sit on the other end of the couch. "You and Xander are close, huh?"

"Close?" Jillian shakes her head. "I wouldn't call it that. I would say, though, that I used to draw hearts on him while he slept and that I was there when he first discovered condoms."

My eyes grow wide.

"He thought they were gloves for thumbs."

I snicker.

"So no, we're not close," Jillian goes on. "We just happen to have this crazy bond even though we're not related by blood..."

My eyebrows shoot up. "You know?"

"Of course I do. I've known all along."

"Oh."

She touches my arm. "You thought it was a secret, didn't you? And you were taking care not to spill it so as not to hurt my feelings, weren't you?"

I don't answer.

"You really are a good person, Robyn." Jillian pats my shoulder. "And seeing what you did with the boys, I'm sure you can handle Xander."

I grin.

"Not to mention you're a natural. You'll be a great mother someday."

Without thinking, I glance at my belly. "You think so?"

"I know so," she answers. "Anyone who can be so good with children who aren't even hers is bound to love her own fiercely."

I smile.

"After all, it isn't easy. I still don't know how Geoffrey and Linda loved me and raised me as their own. Why, some people even throw their own children out the window. And sometimes, I can't blame them. Being a parent is a huge responsibility, and while no one is ever prepared for it, no one should be forced into it."

Forced.

The word immediately makes me think of Xander.

Isn't that what I'm doing? Forcing him to marry me and be the father of my baby? Am I not being unfair to him?

Yes, he offered to help me. He's a good man. But can I really drag him into this? Can I really take advantage of his kindness?

My hand goes to my tummy.

What if Xander realizes he's not ready to be a father? What if he resents the baby and me for forcing him to be?

"Is something wrong?" Jillian asks. "Stomach ache?"

"I'm fine," I assure her.

"The boys didn't make you eat anything gross, did they?"

"Nope." I shake my head. "They made me watch videos, though."

Jillian gives me an expression of sympathetic disgust.

I place my hand over hers. "I'm sure Linda and Geoffrey fell in love with you because you gave them no other choice."

Jillian smiles and squeezes my hand. "You know what? I have a feeling you and I are going to be good friends."

A smile forms on my lips.

"And as your new friend, let me tell you that you're going to love the balloons that I ordered for your wedding, and the butterflies and the..."

~

Friends, huh?

A smile remains glued to my lips as I climb up the spiral staircase.

I haven't had a friend in a while, not since Mom, Dad and Wesley died. I've forgotten how friendship feels, but I suppose it does feel nice.

I mustn't get used to it, though.

When Jillian finds out the truth, I'm sure she's never going to talk to me again.

The notion makes my smile vanish. The memory of her words earlier sends me deep into thought.

Am I really doing the right thing here?

I'm still thinking about it when I come across Geoffrey in the balcony. He seems to be in a pinch; the crease of his eyebrows above the frame of his glasses is adding to the wrinkles on his forehead. He lifts a laptop to peer into the sides, then lifts it higher to look at the bottom before letting it down on the table with a grunt.

I approach him slowly. "Can I help?"

He looks at me. "Ah, Robyn. I thought you were with the boys."

"I was, but it's Jillian's shift now."

Geoffrey grins and lifts his glasses. "You still seem to be in one piece."

I look at my arms and under them. "Yeah. No missing parts."

He chuckles.

I sit on the wicker chair beside him. "So how can I help?"

"I'm afraid I'm just not familiar with these things." He slides his laptop over in front of me. "Strange, huh?

I build houses, but I can't quite figure something this simple out."

"Well, for one, it's not simple."

I push the screen back just a little.

"And two, you just need someone to show you the ropes." I turn to him. "Now, what exactly do you need this baby to do?"

Geoffrey shrugs. "I just want to turn up the volume of the song I'm listening to."

I nod. "Okay."

I place my fingers on the track pad and drag the cursor to the bottom left corner of the screen. I let it hover above the speaker icon.

"See this speaker? You just have to click it." I tap the pad.

"Left or right?"

"Left," I answer. "And by the way, when people say click, the default is left click. If they want you to right click, they'll tell you."

"Noted."

"Then you just have to slide this bar to adjust the volume."

I drag the bar up and down.

He moves his face closer to the screen. "I see."

"Or you could just press some keys." I lean back and point to the keyboard. "Look for the FN key and the key that has the speaker icon. There are usually two."

I point to the speaker icon with the sound waves. "This will increase the volume, and that one without the sound waves will decrease it."

"Ah. And here I thought those keys were useless."

"You just have to make sure you press the FN first and hold it while you're pressing the other key or it won't work. And you have to press the other key a few times before you'll notice much difference."

I slide the laptop back to him. "Now you try it."

He holds down the FN key and taps F3 until the volume is at 70.

"Now play your song," I tell him.

He clicks the play icon on the YouTube video and the song 'El Paso' by Marty Robbins plays.

I smile. "My dad used to love that song."

Geoffrey glances at me. "Did he?"

I nod. "My mom liked rock and pop songs, but my Dad, he loved country. They never fought about that, though."

Geoffrey pats my knee. "I'm sorry to hear he won't be able to walk you down the aisle."

I nod.

I never did think of that tragic consequence until now.

"Xander doesn't have a father, either, you know."

"I know."

"But in his case, it's not so bad. My brother was never cut out to be a father."

I remember the cigarette burns and frown.

He shakes his head. "But the real tragedy was that neither his mother nor I could protect him."

I place my hand over his. "At least you took care of him."

He nods and smiles faintly. The smile widens as his gaze falls on my hand.

"Linda's ring." He touches it. "I remember the day I bought that like it was yesterday. Back then, it cost me nearly my entire fortune."

I lift my hand and stroke the golden band. "You chose well."

"She said she'd let our daughter wear it someday, and Jillian did. And now you." He squeezes my hand. "I have two daughters now."

Warmth swells in my chest all the way up to my throat.

"You know, I would be honored to walk you down the aisle," Geoffrey continues.

My eyes grow wide.

"That is, if you'd like."

I swallow the lump in my throat and blink back the tears.

"That would be priceless."

~

A tear trickles down my cheek and lands on top of my knee as I sit on the edge of the pool. The water shivers as I move my legs back and forth. The ripples distort my reflection, but when I stop moving I can clearly see the lonely pair of eyes staring back at me.

What am I doing? I didn't think this through.

I thought Xander and I wouldn't be hurting anyone, that we'd be the only ones involved, but now Geoffrey is, too. And Jillian. And Linda.

What will they all think when they find out I'm using Xander? What excuses can I give them? None.

I'm a terrible, selfish person.

"So this is where you were," Xander's voice breaks into my thoughts.

I quickly wipe my tear away.

"Are you crying... again?"

I sniff. "No."

He sits beside me. His feet make a small splash as they break the water's surface.

"Are these hormonal tears or emotional?"

I don't answer.

"Did the boys play a prank on you?"

I narrow my eyes at him. "You think I can't handle two kids?"

"Did Jillian say something, then?"

"You mean apart from telling me that you used to wear condoms on your thumbs?"

Xander frowns. "I'll get her for that."

I chuckle. "Jillian may be bossy..."

"She *is* bossy."

"But she's actually nice. She cares a lot about you. And we could have been good friends if I wasn't lying to her."

"Robyn..."

I face him. "Maybe we shouldn't do this after all, Xander."

"You mean call off the wedding?" He shakes his head. "Not happening. We've already talked about this. This is the best thing to..."

"Best for who, exactly?" I ask him.

"For the baby," Xander answers. "For you. For me."

My eyebrows crease. "How is it best for you?"

"Well, for one, it makes Linda happy. She's been worried about me never having a family of my own."

I shake my head. "But you're not the father."

"She doesn't know that. And I don't mind."

"Maybe you should," I tell him. "Maybe you shouldn't let me use you."

He places his hand over mine. "You're not using me, Robyn. I chose this."

"It's not right that you're sacrificing so much."

"That's my choice."

"And what about Jillian? She has no choice but to like me and then be disappointed. And Geoffrey. What if he gets a heart attack or something?"

"Geoffrey is healthy as a horse." Xander squeezes my hand. "They'll understand."

I pull my hand away. "See, that's the problem. You're all such good people. You don't deserve to be caught up in my mess."

"You're a good person, too, Robyn." He touches my cheek. "You deserve to be safe and happy and taken care of."

I fall silent.

He strokes my cheek. "You deserve a family."

My heart stops and my breath catches. Fresh tears sting at the back of my eyes.

I push his hand away. "I don't deserve your family. Or you."

"Because you think I'm so perfect?"

I don't answer.

He grasps my chin so I can look straight into his green-gold eyes. "I'm not, Robyn. I'm not the man you think I am."

"You're a good man," I tell him. "You deserve better than me."

"Really? Well, would a good man do this?"

He pulls me close, reaches around me and gives my butt a squeeze.

"Xan—"

His lips cut off my protest. My breath escapes me.

He pulls away. "See. I'm the one taking advantage of you."

I shake my head but say nothing.

Again, he grasps my chin. "Don't worry about anything, okay? Just think of the baby and the wedding. Jillian tells me it's going to be the best wedding ever on short notice, not to mention the most expensive."

I chuckle. "If anyone can pull it off, it's her."

Xander holds my hand. "That's better. No more tears or cold feet, okay?"

I glance at my feet beneath the water. "Well, my feet are getting kind of cold. But don't worry, I'm not going to be a runaway bride."

"Good." He stands up and offers me his hand. "Because I don't want to be standing alone at the altar."

Chapter Sixteen

Xander

I adjust my black bow tie as I stand in front of the gazebo that has been converted into an altar. The soft breeze caresses my freshly shaved chin. A petal falls from beneath a butterfly in the cage above me and lands on my shoulder.

I brush it off. My gaze meets that of Austin, who's standing a few feet away in an ivory tuxedo. He gives me a toothless smile.

Beside him, Maverick, in an identical tuxedo, stares at his polished shoes as he moves his feet from side to side. Matt, Jillian's husband, stands at the end of the row with phone in hand.

I turn my head to look at the crowd. Most of the benches in front of me are already fully occupied by a sea of tuxedos, dresses and hats. Relatives and close friends only; still, they number over fifty.

Linda sits on the first row in an emerald green dress with sleeves shaped like leaves. I catch the glint of excitement in her eyes peeking from beneath a pink derby hat.

There are other familiar faces in the crowd—Joel and his wife, Shannon, Linda's friends, including Carol, a few neighbors whose houses Geoffrey also designed, some former clients who became friends, old business associates. There are also a few that I don't recognize.

And one that seems to be missing—or so I think until I glimpse a dark-skinned man in his mid-thirties walking towards the last row.

I grin.

So he made it—Tyrone, the only old friend I invited. I was at his wedding, and he was my closest friend back when I was at my old job, so I thought it was only right to invite him. Besides, there's something I'd like to ask Ty.

I crane my neck in an effort to catch his attention, but suddenly the music starts playing. I stand up straight and direct my gaze to the end of the aisle.

Jillian appears first. She's the maid of honor, after all, and she looks positively radiant in her glittering pink gown, outshone only by the diamond necklace around her neck.

I glance to the side and see Matt's eyebrows arch in pleasant surprise. The corner of his mouth twitches up in an approving grin.

Jillian's eyes meet mine briefly as she passes in front of me before heading to her post. Then my gaze pivots to the woman on Geoffrey's arm.

Robyn.

I almost fail to recognize her because of her make-up, but there's no way I can miss those brown eyes gleaming behind the veil or those fiery locks that have been harnessed into a crown studded with flowers on the top of her head.

With each step she takes, the hem of her white gown rustles against the red carpet. The toes of her shoes peek out from underneath.

A bouquet of pink orchids and white lilies sits tightly in the grip of one of her hands right between her breasts. I can glimpse their curves above her beaded sweetheart neckline. The emerald engagement ring glistens on her other hand, which is clutching Geoffrey's arm. Her bare shoulders are squared if not a little stiff.

As Robyn passes by Linda's seat, Linda stands up to give her a hug and a kiss on both cheeks. Robyn slips the ring off her finger and hands it to her.

Geoffrey also kisses Robyn on the cheek before taking his seat beside his wife. Robyn steps forward alone.

As she lifts her head, our eyes meet for the first time. My breath catches. My heart holds still beneath my boutonniere.

I walk towards her and offer her my hand. As our fingers touch, my heart begins to pound. Her hand quivers.

I grasp it in mine and lead her up the steps of the gazebo to the altar where the parson has been waiting.

"You sure took your time," I whisper as I tuck her arm in mine. "For a moment there, I got scared you might have stood me up."

"I told you I'd be here," she whispers back.

I smile. "You look beautiful."

The corners of her lips curve up as well. "You shaved."

The parson clears his throat. "Dearly beloved, we are gathered here together on this beautiful, blessed day to witness the union of…"

~

"Congratulations!" Joel shakes my hand firmly before pulling me in for a pat on the shoulder. "And welcome to the club."

"When Joel first told me about it, I didn't believe him," his wife, Shannon, says. "But I do now."

"Yup." I show her the golden band on my finger. "I'm a married man."

"A happily married man, I should think." Shannon pats my shoulder as well. "And you know how you can stay that way? Listen to your wife."

She glances at Robyn, who Linda is still introducing to her friends.

"Oh, is that so?" Joel gives her a puzzled look.

"It is so." Shannon nudges Joel in the ribs.

"Ouch." Joel rubs them.

Shannon sniffs and turns around. "I smell something good from the buffet table."

"Please help yourself," I encourage.

"I think I will." Shannon walks off.

Joel sighs. "You'd think that after nearly twenty years of marriage, I'd get some respect."

I respond to the remark with a chuckle before turning serious. "You didn't tell her anything?"

Joel was the one person I confided in, not just because I trusted him but because I couldn't hide the marriage from him. And since he's seen Robyn from the start, he knows the marriage is fake. I didn't want him questioning it.

"Of course not," he answers. "I told the boys to keep their mouths shut, too."

"Thanks." This time, I pat his shoulder. "I knew I could count on you."

He lifts a finger. "You owe me one, though."

"I owe you a lot," I correct him.

"Well, just make sure things turn out fine," he tells me. "Since you told me this was the right thing to do."

"I will," I promise him as I glance in Tyrone's direction.

Joel glances at the buffet table.

"I better make sure Shannon doesn't eat too much or she'll get mad at me later. She says she gained weight because I wasn't around to tell her when to stop eating. If you ask me, I think it's because she eats as many chips and chocolates as the kids, but don't tell her I said that."

"I won't."

Joel walks away and I head towards Tyrone—only to have Jillian stop me midway.

"Ah, the maid of honor." I give her a hug.

"You can thank me for everything later," Jillian says. "For now, there's someone I want you to meet."

She turns to the woman behind her, a woman in her fifties with a mole above the left corner of her mouth.

"This is Connie Thompson. Have you heard of her?"

I shake my head.

"She says she used to work with your mother," Jillian explains.

My eyebrows arch.

"Xander's mom?" Robyn asks as she joins us.

Connie nods. "We worked at the same hospital and in the same department. We were on the same shift most of the time."

I touch my chin and look away. My mother rarely talked about work, mostly because she was too busy with chores once she got home. And I never asked. But I suppose it isn't unlikely.

I turn my gaze back to Connie. She looks about the same age Mom would have been if she were still alive. Also, she doesn't seem to be lying.

But why is she here?

"I wanted your mother to have a representative at your wedding," Jillian explains. "So I tracked her friends down. Matt helped."

Trust Jillian to get everything covered.

"I'm sure your mother is smiling down on you right now," Connie tells me before turning to Robyn. "And, of course, on you, too, dear."

Robyn smiles. "I sure hope so."

"I thought about buying you a present, but then, I remembered that there was something Rachel gave me that I could give to you." Connie hands Robyn a silver box with a white bow.

Robyn stares at the box. "Something from Xander's mother?"

"Open it," Jillian urges.

Robyn nods and pulls the ribbon. Then she takes off the lid of the box to reveal the rainbow-colored blanket inside.

"Rachel knitted this for me shortly after I had a miscarriage." Connie pulls the blanket out of the box. "She had no doubt I'd have another child, a healthy baby, and sure enough, I ended up with not just one but three. They're all grown now."

Robyn runs her fingers over the wool. "It's beautiful."

"I thought I'd give it to you since, well, I no longer need it," Connie says. "Besides, I believe it brought me good luck, especially where children are concerned. Who knows? It might do the same for you."

Robyn folds the blanket. "But this must mean so much to you."

Connie shakes her head. "I have my rainbow children. You keep the blanket. Use it and hand it over to your children."

She turns to me.

"I'm sure that's what Rachel would have wanted."

I say nothing.

Robyn presses the folded blanket to her heart. Her eyes brim with tears.

"Thank you so much."

Connie smiles. "You're welcome."

Jillian places an arm around Robyn. "Hey, don't cry. You'll ruin your makeup, and there are still lots of pictures to be taken."

But it's too late. Tears are already streaking down Robyn's pink cheeks, washing away every fragment of cosmetics in their path.

Jillian frowns and grabs Robyn's hand. "Come with me."

She whisks my wife away, leaving me alone with Connie.

"I'm sorry," she apologizes before I can.

I shake my head. "It's not your fault. Women get emotional at weddings, don't they?"

Especially if they're pregnant.

"True," Connie agrees. "I cried at my own wedding, too. And my daughter cried at hers. I believe that women who cry at their weddings end up with happy endings."

"Interesting."

Just then, I spot Tyrone walking towards me.

"Thank you again," I tell Connie as I pat her shoulder. "And please excuse me."

"Of course."

I meet Tyrone halfway and offer him my hand. "Hey."

"Hey yourself, man." He shakes my hand firmly. "Alexander Bolt, finally in love and married. I had to see it to believe it."

"That seems to be the common sentiment," I reply. "Anyway, I'm glad you came, Ty."

He puts his arm around me. "Are you kidding? We haven't seen each other for years. Why waste the opportunity?"

I lead him away from the crowd. "Actually, I'm glad you came because I have a favor to ask you."

Tyrone's eyebrows go up. "Okay…"

"I want you to find out what you can about a man named Howard Mitchell."

This time, his eyebrows crease. "Why?"

"Let's just say he and Robyn have a nasty history and I want that deleted," I answer.

"Okay." Tyrone nods. "But you know I'm a cop, right? Not a hit man."

"I know. I'm not asking you to kill him. I'm asking you to find dirt on him so he can be locked away forever and he'll never bother Robyn again."

Tyrone touches his chin. "What kind of dirt are we talking about?"

"Drugs. Sexual assault. Maybe even sex trafficking. Attempted homicide. Theft. Coercion. Gang-related crimes."

Tyrone lets out a whistle.

I pat his back. "Anyway, I'm sure you'll find something."

He nods. "Well, if he's as bad as you say he is, then it's my job to put him away."

"But don't tell anyone, okay?" I ask him.

Another nod. "You know you can trust me, pal."

"I know. That's why I asked you."

Tyrone sighs. "And here I thought you invited me to your wedding because I'm your best friend."

"You are," I tell him. "And you're also the best cop I know."

Tyrone grins. "Man, I've missed you, but I'm glad to see you're—"

"Alex!" A woman's voice rises above the chatter of the crowd in the garden.

I turn my head to see a woman with a strawberry blonde bob marching towards me in a white dress and thigh-high black boots. The crowd parts for her with murmurs erupting from either side.

Great. The last person I wanted to see at my wedding.

I go to her. "Tracy, what are you doing here?"

"Trying to stop your wedding, obviously," she answers.

"How did you even know I was getting married?" I ask her curiously.

"The photographer you hired happens to be a friend of a friend," Tracy explains.

Tyrone breaks the news. "Tracy, you never could show up on time for anything. The ceremony is already over, so you came all the way for nothing and you should just leave."

Tracy's eyes grow wide with shock. She drops the purse she's clutching and beats her fists against my chest. "How could you? I've been waiting for you to call me all this time."

The murmurs grow into chatter. I grab Tracy's arms and lead her away from the crowd. Tyrone follows us.

As soon as we're behind the gazebo, she wrenches her arms free.

"Do you have any idea how hurt I was when you just disappeared?" Tracy puts her hand on her chest. "Then I heard about the fire and I thought you were dead. I mourned for you."

"Well, as you can see, I'm alive," I tell her. "And I'm married."

She glances at the ring on my finger. "You could have at least called me to say goodbye. I loved you."

My jaw clenches. "You have no idea how much your love cost me."

"Because I turned off your phone?" She beats her hand against her chest. "I saved your life, Alex. If not for me—"

I cut her off. "I think you've said enough."

Tracy shakes her head. "Alex, you—"

"I believe we asked you to leave." Tyrone steps forward. "If you don't, I'll have to arrest you for trespassing and disturbing the peace."

"Disturbing the peace, huh?" Tracy snorts. "Why should he have peace when I haven't had any for the past six years?"

She kicks a flower pot, cracking it.

"Tracy," Tyrone warns sternly.

She sinks to the ground and lets out a wail, then breaks into sobs.

I frown.

"What's going on?" Robyn asks as she comes out of the house.

I quickly go to her after throwing Tyrone a glance to let him know I'm leaving Tracy in his capable hands.

"Alex, don't leave me!" Tracy wails.

I ignore her.

"I did nothing wrong! I saved your life, damn it!"

"Who's that?" Robyn asks with furrowed eyebrows as I approach her.

"No one." I turn her around and lead her back into the house.

Robyn glances over her shoulder. "Is she your ex?"

"Yes," I confess. "But you don't have to worry about her. She's out of her mind. Tyrone is getting rid of her now."

"Why was she so upset?"

"She can't accept the fact that I'm married." I pull Robyn up the stairs.

"I should have known one of your exes would show up," she mutters.

I turn to her. "You're not jealous, are you, Mrs. Bolt?"

Robyn doesn't answer.

"It doesn't matter," I assure her as I touch her cheek. "You're my wife now."

She glances around. "Fake wife."

I frown, then lift her into my arms.

"Xander!" she squeals.

I carry her over the threshold and set her down with a mischievous grin. "I have a very real wedding night planned for us, though."

Chapter Seventeen

Robyn

I suck a deep breath into my lungs as I stare at my reflection in the bathroom mirror.

Now that my hair is flowing freely again—i.e., back to being a mess—and the eyeliner, cheek tint and lipstick have all been washed off, I can finally recognize myself.

I touch my cheek and let my fingers slide down to my neck.

Yup. This is the real me, not the me who's been putting on an act to convince everyone I'm marrying for love and not just because I'm carrying the baby of a maniac.

The ring on my finger, the most important accessory I now possess, gleams.

Now, that's no fake.

I take off the golden band and hold it up to the light, which reveals the name engraved on the inside.

Xander.

I still can't believe he's my husband now.

A smile coats my lips as I remember how dashing he looked in his crisp, perfectly tailored, charcoal black tuxedo. Not to mention with his chin neatly shaved and his hair trimmed short.

I've never minded the extra hair. I thought the rugged, rough around the edges look made Xander look more manly. After seeing him without it, though, I can understand why so many women have fallen for him.

Like that Tracy.

I can't believe she had the guts to show up at our wedding.

Well, I can't believe a friend of Xander's mom showed up, either, though that was a pleasant surprise.

"Robyn, are you alright?" Xander asks from the other side of the bathroom door.

"I'm okay," I assure him as I slip the ring back on.

I don't want to lose it, after all.

"I'll be out in a bit."

"If you say so."

I turn my gaze back to the mirror.

There's one more thing I can't believe—this... thing I'm wearing.

The black satin which hugs the curves of my breasts hangs from thin, golden braids around my shoulders. The cups are held together in the middle of my chest by a gold ring. From the bottom curves, wisps of sheer black chiffon flow and billow around my waist over a black lace thong. Gold straps bridge the seams of the underwear to the embroidered garters of a pair of thigh-high black stockings.

Seriously, what's the point of wearing stockings at home? Or of wearing panties that give you wedgies? Or of wearing clothes that don't cover anything, for that matter?

I know, I know. That's the lure of lingerie. But honestly, I don't understand it. I've never worn a piece until today. I've never even considered spending hard-earned money on it. (That's another mystery—why they're so expensive when they're constructed of barely any fabric.)

Still, tonight is my wedding night, so I guess it's the perfect opportunity to try something new. Also, it's Xander's wedding gift, so I have no choice but to wear it.

Too bad I didn't get him a present, too, but when I mentioned it, he simply said that this... outfit was a present for both of us.

Oh well. If that's the case, then it's time we both enjoy our present.

I take another deep breath before opening the door. My feet leave the cold marble tiles and land on the soft beige carpet.

Only my footsteps make a sound in the quiet bedroom. Only the glow of the bedside lamp pierces the darkness, spilling onto the carpet and the bed.

And a very naked Xander.

His back is against the velvet headboard, his arms folded behind his head like a cushion. His long legs are sprawled out in front of him, his ankles crossed. The shadows of his muscles contrast with his pale skin.

My breath catches. My nipples stiffen against the satin. Butterflies flutter in my stomach beneath the cloak of chiffon.

When my gaze wanders between Xander's legs where his thick cock is standing at attention, I feel heat blossom between my legs. Nectar spills out and seeps into the lace.

I pull my gaze up to his face and my heart stops as I see the scorching desire in his eyes. I have no doubt it mirrors mine.

Xander hooks a finger at me, and I walk towards him like a puppy eager to please.

"It's unfair," I point out as I climb onto the bed on fours. "I'm wearing something and you're not wearing anything."

He grins. "Unfair to who, exactly?"

I answer by brushing my fingers along the length of his cock.

He inhales sharply. "I seem to be at a disadvantage."

I climb up his legs and straddle him.

"Shall I take this thing off, then?"

I reach for a bra strap.

"No." His hand goes over mine. "I like it."

My eyes narrow. "You do?"

He answers by grabbing one of my breasts with his mouth. Moisture and heat penetrate the silk. His lips clamp on an engorged nipple and I gasp.

"I can't decide if you look ravishing in it or it looks ravishing on you," Xander says as he pulls away.

His hands crawl up my thighs and rest on my butt. His nails bite into the mounds of flesh. I shiver.

"And I can't decide if I like you better with or without your beard." I run my knuckles across his jaw and press my lips against the smooth skin of his chin.

He grips mine and slides my mouth over to his. The tip of his tongue traces the oval formed by my lips before it barges past them. I trap it to give it a light suck before allowing it to play with my tongue. Heat ripples in my chest with every thunderous beat of my heart.

Xander's fingers dance across the bare skin of my back as mine get lost in his hair. I start moving my hips. The leaking tip of his cock moistens the crack of my ass while the lace covering the front grows even wetter. I moan into his mouth.

He breaks the kiss to plant his lips below my ear. They trail down to my neck, then follow my collarbone towards the middle. His mouth descends into the valley between my aching breasts and his tongue darts out to lick the patch of skin inside the golden ring.

My breasts ache even more. Their peaks strain against the satin.

When Xander unclasps the gold ring and pushes it off, they finally jerk free. But not for long.

Xander imprisons one between his lips and takes the other hostage between his fingers. My moans turn into cries.

I lean forward and cradle his head as he plays with my breasts. The ache and the heat travel lower, past my belly to my core. It swells and the stain on the black lace grows larger.

Unable to hold back my desire, I grab Xander's hand and slip it beneath my soaked underwear. His fingers find my nub and my palms flatten against the wall. My nails rake the velvet.

His hand strokes me as his lips and tongue keep my nipples occupied and excited. I throw my head back as I gasp for oxygen between whimpers.

The heat in my body, fueled by rioting hormones, begs for release. With every lick of that wicked tongue, every press of those fingers against the sensitive bud that's now in full bloom, I get closer and closer to the edge.

I fall.

I clutch Xander's shoulders as the pleasure sends my veins exploding. A loud cry erupts from my mouth as the breath gets knocked out of my lungs. My body quakes all over, on the brink of shattering.

Afterwards, I collapse against him as I catch my breath. The twitching cock beneath me warns that the reprieve will not be long.

Sure enough, after just a few moments, Xander kisses me again. Then he pushes me off him so that I'm back on my hands and knees on the bed.

Fingers travel up the silken trail at the back of my legs. They take refuge at the back of my knees and I hold back a laugh at the tickling sensation.

Strange, but in spite of the silk—or maybe because of the silk—his touches seem to excite me more.

His lips descend on my ass. They part and teeth playfully nip at one cheek.

He pulls the drenched floss of fabric and rubs it against my crack. Then he pushes it aside and teases my hole.

I hold my breath as I feel that ring of muscle quiver, afraid of what Xander might try next. He's only teasing, though, and his fingers move on to slip inside me.

I gasp and gather handfuls of the sheets beneath me. My head falls forward. My knees wobble.

He moves his fingers in and out and I moan against the sheets. A puddle of saliva forms beneath me.

Those fingers reach in deeply and I cry out. My toes curl and I move my hips against him.

"Xander," I hiss out his name.

"Yes, Mrs. Bolt?"

"Just fuck me already, Mr. Bolt," I order.

The fingers grow still. "Are you ordering me around?"

"Please," I whisper.

"Well, Joel's wife did tell me I should listen to my wife if I wanted to be happy."

"She di—?"

His fingers push in deeply one last time before departing. I glance back and find Xander kneeling behind me. His hands grip my hips.

"Here I go."

That's all the warning I get before he sheathes his cock inside me to the hilt. My mouth gapes open and my fingers grip the sheets.

"Are you okay?" Xander asks hoarsely.

I nod.

"Just tell me if it's too rough," he says. "I don't want to hurt you."

"Just fuck me," I repeat.

And Xander obeys. He begins pounding into me, rocking my body with each thrust. The golden straps slip off my shoulders. My breasts dance and my nipples graze the cotton. The chiffon rustles and the bed creaks.

Then Xander gives a particularly hard thrust. I scream as a second orgasm is wrenched from my trembling body along with my supply of air. His nails dig into my hips as he empties himself deep inside me. His own hips jerk and his cock pulses.

Then he goes completely still before pulling out. I feel a warm trail snake down my thigh just before I collapse on my side. My hair falls over my face.

To my surprise, Xander pulls my limp body into his arms. I rest my head against his chest and he pulls the blanket over our legs.

"How's your tummy?" he asks.

I glance down at my belly hiding beneath the chiffon. The bump isn't noticeable yet, but I can already tell the swell of the curve has grown.

"It's okay," I assure him.

I notice that my breasts are still sticking out, although they no longer ache and my nipples have softened.

"You know, I still don't understand why you told me to wear this." I run my fingers over the chiffon. "Wasn't it just in the way?"

"No," he answers as he cups one of my bare breasts. His hot breath tickles my ear. "You liked it, too. Admit it."

I don't. Not out loud.

Mentally, though, I finally understand why women wear lingerie. There's something thrilling about being fucked while still clothed but not covered entirely. Then there's the luxurious and sensual feel of the delicate fabric that makes you feel more like a woman.

"Well?" Xander asks as his fingers stroke my hair.

I turn my head to meet his gaze. "I'll answer your question if you answer mine."

"Okay."

I swallow a gulp of air before blurting out the question that's been weighing on my mind. "What was it that Tracy did that she said wasn't her fault? And does it have something to do with your unforgivable mistake?"

"That's two questions," Xander says.

I know, but I just had to seize the tenderness of the moment and ask.

"Tracy turned off my phone and I missed an important call," he finally confides. "Because of that, I lost my job and my friends."

I frown. "She said she saved you."

"She didn't," he tells me without a doubt.

"She said that it's not her fault. Why do you think it's yours?"

"You shouldn't pay attention to anything she said," he answers. "And I should have been more careful. More responsible."

"More wary of women," I add.

He nods and kisses the top of my head. "Now, you answer my question. Do you like wearing something like this?"

He takes a strap between his teeth and pulls.

I snuggle into the crook of his shoulder and smile. "It's not so bad."

And who knows? Maybe neither is getting married.

Maybe, just maybe, I finally have a chance to get on with my life.

Chapter Eighteen

Howie

I can't go on without Robyn.

The realization, reached after weeks of fruitless searching, fucking nameless girls and alternating between gin and Xanax, sends my fist flying into the nearest wall. The wood splits beneath my knuckles and the crackle travels across the room.

Of course, the sound of bone shattering from my punch would have been more satisfying, but I've already punched Vaughn and Tom and Ian for their slip-up. I would have punched them some more, until they ended up as piles of maggot-infested flesh and bone fragments at the bottom of a ditch, but I still need them.

I still need them to help me find Robyn.

I ignore my bleeding hand and sink into a black leather armchair.

How Robyn managed to escape remains a mystery to me. She didn't have any clothes on. She had bruises. Someone kept an eye on her at all times, except during bathroom breaks. The window in the bathroom was so tiny I didn't think she'd fit through it.

Obviously, I was wrong.

It's even more baffling how she was able to evade the clutches of three ex-soldiers turned mercenaries. Or how she was able to go so far through the woods.

One of the reasons why I brought her to this particular cabin was because it was in the middle of nowhere. No neighbors. Far from the road. Heck, there's barely even any cellphone reception.

And still, she escaped.

From the middle of nowhere, Robyn was able to go somewhere out of my reach.

I tap my fingers on the arm of the chair and grin.

As pissed as I am, I have to admit I'm impressed by Robyn's guts and cleverness. Then again, I always knew she was smart and fierce.

That's what makes her so interesting.

And so much fun to bend to my will, if not break, in the same way my stepmother broke me.

Just the thought of Robyn naked and tied up, biting her lower lip to keep her cries from coming out and doing her best not to tremble beneath my touches, sends blood rushing to my crotch. My cock stiffens in my briefs.

I close my eyes and draw in a deep breath as I suppress a shiver.

I may not have broken Robyn yet, but that's precisely why I have to get her back.

I lean forward and join the tips of my fingers. The tip of my tongue brushes against my lips.

I will get Robyn back.

And when I do, I'm going to carve myself into every fiber of her being so that she can never run away from me again.

Chapter Nineteen

Robyn

The inside of Dr. Evelyn Strafford's waiting room reminds me of an Easter egg hunt.

Strips of pastel colors, some with zigzag lines or spirals, coat the walls, while all the pieces of furniture are eggshell white like the floor. Oval shelves have been carved out of the wall to hold wicker baskets of plastic flowers and books. A jar of colorful jelly beans sits in the middle of the coffee table. There's even a mother bunny huddled in a fenced corner surrounded by a dozen baby bunnies.

If not for the sign on the door and the receptionist's desk surrounded by filing cabinets in the opposite corner, I wouldn't have thought we were in a doctor's waiting room.

But that is where we are, and that is what we are doing—waiting.

For my part, waiting anxiously.

Beside me, Xander sits calmly as he does something on his phone. The other two women in the room don't seem nervous, either. One of them is watching the rerun of *Grey's Anatomy* on the wall-mounted TV and the other one's snacking on some fruit slices.

I pretend I'm occupied with last month's issue of *Parenting* magazine which is sprawled on my lap, but in truth I've been stuck on the same page for minutes now. My heart won't stop hammering in my chest in a double-time counterpoint to the ticking of the bunny-eared clock on the wall, which I glance at every now and then.

I can't help it.

Even though this is already my third prenatal check-up and Xander is at my side once again, today is an important day.

Today, I'm going to find out if I'm having a boy or a girl.

More importantly, today, I'm going to see my baby for the first time and the fact that I'm a mother will finally sink in.

Everything is about to get more real.

And more scary.

"Hey." Xander takes my hand. "Everything is going to be alright."

I just nod.

I don't even trust myself to speak, knowing I might stammer or that my teeth might even chatter.

Just then, the door to Dr. Strafford's office opens and a woman older than me and with a bigger bump—she's probably in her third trimester—waddles out.

The receptionist whose name I still haven't asked for stands up. "Mrs. Bolt?"

I don't move.

Xander squeezes my hand. "That's you."

"Oh, right."

I'm still not used to being called that, especially by other people.

I slip the magazine back into the rack and stand up. I smooth the front of my yellow maternity dress and follow the receptionist inside the office. Xander follows me with my purse in hand.

"Robyn."

Dr. Strafford's maroon lips curve into a smile that I nervously return.

One of Linda's friends recommended her, and I'm truly grateful. Dr. Stafford may be in her forties, but she has the bubbly warmth of a woman in her twenties, the confidence of a woman in her thirties and the wisdom of a woman in her fifties. Plus, I like her candy-colored clothes and her funky jewelry, which do not at all take away from her medical expertise that's proven by the numerous plaques and framed certificates hanging on the wall behind her.

"Thanks for seeing us again, Dr. Strafford," Xander says as he takes his seat across from me.

"The pleasure is always mine." She goes over my file on her desk. "Now, let's see. We're 22 weeks along, aren't we?"

She glances at the calendar on her desk, then turns to me.

"How are you feeling, Robyn?"

"Good," I answer as I fidget with my dress. "Better than last month."

True, I seem to be more tired now, but I'm also getting dizzy and nauseous less often.

"Good." Dr. Strafford gives me a wide smile. "That means everything's on track. So I guess you're ready for your ultrasound?"

I nod, even though I'm not really sure.

"Brenda," Dr. Strafford calls out and a woman in a nurse's uniform appears behind the curtain. "Get Mrs. Bolt ready, will you?"

Brenda nods and offers me her hand. "Please come with me."

I follow her past the green curtain where the bed is.

"Please pull your dress up and lie down on the bed," Brenda instructs.

I obey. The cotton bunches up just below my bra. Brenda rolls down the garter of my underwear as well, then covers my lower half with a blanket.

"Now, this is going to be cold," she says before squirting some liquid on my tummy.

It is cold, and I wince as she rubs it around. It feels sticky, too.

The curtain parts again and Dr. Stafford enters, Xander in tow.

My eyebrows arch.

Well, that's a surprise. Xander usually stays on the other side of the curtain.

"Now, let's see this bun in the oven, huh?" Dr. Strafford says as she sits on the stool by the bed.

Brenda hands her a device connected to the machine that reminds me of a flat, plastic microphone and she holds it against my tummy.

I feel a slight pressure.

"Eyes on the screen," Dr. Strafford tells me as she moves the device around.

I direct my gaze to the small black and white screen. At first, I don't see anything but blotches. Then my heart stops as I see a distinct white silhouette.

My baby.

"There's the head." Dr. Strafford points out. "And the feet. Nothing out of the ordinary."

I let out a sigh of relief.

"And I don't see a penis, which means..."

It's a girl.

The image of a young girl with red pigtails and bright eyes pops into my head and warmth flows into my chest.

"Mr. and Mrs. Bolt, meet your daughter."

I stare at the screen as my eyes brim with tears. Then my lips curve into a smile, all my nervousness gone.

All I feel now is thrill and awe and a fierce sense of pride and protectiveness that takes me by surprise.

My daughter.

A hand covers mine and I glance to my side to see Xander also beaming with pride.

Like me, he seems to have fallen in love at first sight.

The fact that I'm sharing this moment with someone else doubles the warmth in my chest instead of diminishing it. Thrill turns to joy.

I squeeze Xander's hand and allow my fingers to entwine with his.

"Well, that's that."

Dr. Strafford freezes the screen before handing the device back to Brenda, who gives me a smile and a wad of tissue.

"Congratulations."

"Of course, you still have a long way to go," Dr. Strafford says. "And Robyn, I want you to..."

I'm no longer listening, though. My eyes remain glued to the image on the screen as I wipe the cold gel off my tummy. My heart beats in my ears.

I'm having a baby girl.

~

"Are you glad it's a girl?" Xander asks me during lunch at a Spanish bistro not far from the hospital. It's another one of Linda's friend's recommendations.

I don't answer at once because I'm busy digging into my pan of Paella Valenciana—yes, pan.

"I am, actually." I wipe a flaxen grain of rice off my cheek with a knuckle. "I always wanted a little sister who I could put pretty dresses on, whose hair I could braid the way I never could mine."

Xander delivers a spoonful of mashed potatoes with chorizo and manchego to his mouth and licks the spoon.

"Didn't your parents buy you a doll?"

"They did." I pull the flesh off a clam and toss it past my lips. "But a doll doesn't look up at you with eyes filled with wonder and adoration."

"True."

I shove another spoonful brimming with yellow grains inside my mouth. "I wouldn't have minded a boy, though. After hanging out with your nephews, I think I'm quite prepared for that."

Xander grins as he sticks his fork into a slice of Bistec Encebollado. "I have no doubt."

He brings it to his mouth and the rich, orange sauce coats his lips.

He wipes it off with a table napkin.

"But you're having a girl. Won't Jillian be jealous?"

I frown, knowing she will be.

Xander reaches for his glass of wine. "And what will you be naming her?"

I shrug and take a sip from my glass of pomegranate juice. "I haven't thought that far ahead yet. Any ideas?"

His eyebrows arch. "You're asking me?"

I give another shrug. "Why not? You're the one who's going to take care of her. Heck, you're already doing it. If you name her, then she'll always have a part of you, don't you think?"

Xander falls silent. His gaze drops to his plate. His utensils go still in his hands.

Did I say something I shouldn't have?

"Of course, if you don't like—"

"I'll think of something," he cuts me off as his eyes meet mine.

"Okay." I eat another spoonful of my paella, the pile topped with a piece of shrimp this time. "Just don't name her after an ex."

His eyes narrow and my eyebrows furrow.

Is he really mad now?

"I'm just saying…"

He pulls the pan away from me.

"Hey," I complain with wide eyes as I grab the opposite handle of the pan. "What are you doing with my paella?"

"Finishing it." He eats a spoonful and my jaw drops. "You heard Dr. Strafford. You shouldn't eat too much."

He swallows.

"Man, this is yummy."

He's about to take another spoonful, but I pull the pan back. "Don't mess with me. Grudges over food may be mad, but believe me, grudges over food with a pregnant woman? You don't want them."

Xander chuckles and raises his hands. "Fine. But don't say I didn't warn you."

I continue eating.

"At least slow down. People will think you haven't been eating."

"With this tummy?" I touch it. "I don't think so."

One of the good things about pregnancy is that I can eat a lot and no one will raise an eyebrow at me because I'm eating for two. And oh, I'm allowed to eat weird food, too, like mashed potatoes with chocolate and dried mangoes with anchovies. That pretty much makes up for the fact that I've had to cut down on coffee and stay away from alcohol entirely.

I glance at Xander's glass of wine with longing.

Well, it won't be long now.

"Well, hurry up then." Xander gobbles up another morsel of his steak. "You did say you couldn't wait to go shopping."

Ah, yes. The dresses. The Wonder Woman headband. The dainty shoes. The onesies that say 'Cute Like Mommy' or 'When I Grow Up, I'm Going To Rule The World'.

I give him a grin. "You better brace yourself. You're about to do some heavy lifting, Mr. Bolt."

Chapter Twenty

Xander

"You sure have gotten heavy."

I let out a grunt as I set Robyn down at the top of the long, creaking staircase.

"You're the one who offered to carry me," she points out.

She smooths the front of her maternity dress—a teal, open-shoulder knee-length dress that she got along with the clothes for the baby last week—and runs her fingers through her hair.

I stare at the door in front of me.

"Close your eyes."

"Xander, what is this about?" she asks.

I glance at her. "Just do it."

She sighs but obeys. "Okay."

As soon as her eyes are closed, I put my hand on the door knob.

"Open your eyes at the count of three. One..."

I open the door and lead her through it.

"Two..."

I turn the lights on.

"Three."

Robyn opens her eyes, which grow wide as she takes in the room.

Last week, Linda and Geoffrey gave me permission to convert the attic into a nursery, and that is exactly what I've done—or asked Caitlin to do.

Watermelon pink wallpaper adorns the walls. A bubblegum pink carpet covers the floor. Rays of sun flow into the room through the skylight and pierce the white gossamer crown canopy to shine right on the taffy-colored sleigh crib.

I would have had a stained glass window installed, knowing Robyn would have loved it, but that would have required tearing down the roof. Even if Linda and Geoffrey gave me their permission, the construction of the window and the installation would have taken weeks. I had to seize the momentum from last week's check-up, so I couldn't afford that long a wait.

Next to the crib, a velvet-lined chair designed like a throne with gold-tasseled fuchsia cushions stands guard. Dolls sit on a shelf amid other feminine trinkets— a pair of tiny ballet slippers, a bamboo fan, glittering, heart-shaped sunglasses atop a folded scarf, a clock held by two unicorns.

Caitlin really outdid herself this time.

There's even a wooden music box on the table by the crib right next to a carousel lamp...

I pause. My eyes grow wide.

"A carousel?" Robyn glares at me. "You know how I feel about carousels."

"Sorry." I go over to the table and pick up the carousel lamp to conceal it behind me. "I must have forgotten to tell Caitlin that..."

"Caitlin?" Robyn's eyebrows furrow even more. "You asked Caitlin to decorate my daughter's nursery?"

Shit. I wasn't going to tell her that.

I draw a deep breath. "I wanted the nursery to be the best, so I hired the best interior designer I knew."

Her hands fall to her hips. "Are you seriously complimenting that bitch right now?"

Wow. She's not mincing words, is she?

I slap my forehead. "Robyn, listen..."

"Well, I feel sorry for Caitlin, but I don't like this nursery. The dolls look like they're from a horror movie."

She grabs one of the porcelain dolls on the shelf and throws it to the floor. Its painted face cracks.

"I don't want my daughter to grow up to be as spoiled as Paris Hilton. God forbid."

She grabs the sunglasses and tosses them into the diaper bin.

I roll my eyes. "Robyn."

She wrenches her hand away and tears down the canopy. "It's too pompous. Like the designer. And so is this chair."

She throws the cushion on the floor and kicks it away.

"And this room is too pink. Why, Dr. Stafford could design a better nursery than this. Maybe you should have asked her to be your interior decorator."

My jaw clenches and I grab her arm before she can grab something else. "Robyn, that's enough."

She grabs the carousel lamp I'm hiding behind me and sends it crashing into a wall. It explodes into pieces.

Then she glares at me and marches off.

I sink down on the throne chair and rub my temples.

What kind of monster have I unleashed? Who even knew Robyn could have such a nasty temper?

Then again, her moods have changed, like they're on an entirely different spectrum, and I knew I was taking a risk by asking Caitlin to design the nursery. I was just hoping Robyn would forgive me for it once she saw the room and fell in love with it.

Clearly, that's not what happened.

And now the nursery is a mess.

I pick up a horse head from the carousel and let out a sigh.

I have to fix this.

~

I find Robyn in Linda's greenhouse after dinner.

She didn't show up at the dinner table to have a taste of Linda's chicken pot pie, and she wasn't there when I returned to the bedroom, so I began searching for her throughout the house and grounds.

The greenhouse has no lights of its own, but by the glow of the strategically positioned backyard lamps, softened by the flicker of tiny wings, I make out a strange shadow among the plants. I go inside and find her admiring the orchids, wearing a lavender robe over her blue pajamas. A large black clip holds the strands of her hair prisoners between its large, curved teeth. Caramel-colored bedroom slippers enclose her toes.

When she sees me, she moves away from the flowers and sits on a bench. Her fingers fidget with the sash of her robe.

I tuck my hands into the pockets of my navy blue sweater and sit beside her.

"You weren't at dinner," I tell her.

"Wasn't hungry," she mumbles.

My eyebrows arch. "That's a first."

Her protruding lower lip jars me back to my senses.

Right. I'm not here to pick another fight.

I turn my head towards her. "Are you okay?"

Robyn's fingers grow still. Her shoulders rise and fall as she sucks in a deep breath.

"I'm sorry about... earlier. I shouldn't have reacted like that."

She seems to have calmed down.

"It's okay," I tell her. "The fault was mine."

"Still, I shouldn't have destroyed those things or made such a mess. I don't know what came over me."

"The hormones?" I suggest.

And maybe the jealousy.

Robyn shakes her head. "It's not just the hormones. It's the whole pregnancy thing. It's... taken over me completely."

She lets out a sigh and stares at the glass ceiling.

"It's just so hard. The back aches. The frequent trips to the bathroom. The constant hunger. The feeling that you've been run over by a truck most of the time and that you're getting bigger and uglier by the day."

"You're not—"

"But you know what's the worst?" She cuts me off as she places her hands on her forehead. "It's being scared all the time, scared that you might be doing something that's not good for your baby, scared that when the baby comes out, you'll lose your shit or worse, you'll lose yourself. Even now, I don't know who I am. What more when the baby comes out?"

I place my hand over hers. "Hey. It's okay. You're going to be okay."

She looks at me and sniffs. "Am I?"

I squeeze her hand. "Maybe the problem is you're fighting the pregnancy. Maybe you should just sit back and enjoy it. It's okay to lose control a little."

Robyn shakes her head. "I feel like I'm losing everything."

"Well, you won't lose me," I tell her. "I told you I was going to take care of you and the baby."

"But you're not even her father," she reminds me. "And you don't love me."

Her mention of the L-word takes me by surprise.

"Now that I'm fat and ugly, I'm sure you'd rather be with someone else. Like Caitlin, for example."

I frown. "You are not fat and—"

"You said yourself that I'm heavy," Robyn points out.

"You are heavier now," I confess. "But that's not a bad thing. I promise I am not going to cheat on you. You may not be my real wife, but I'm not going to embarrass or hurt you like that."

She looks away.

I exhale.

Alright. If she doesn't believe my words, I'll just have to assuage her fears through actions.

I move closer to Robyn and take her face between my hands. I press my lips to hers. As she gasps, I push my tongue in. She shivers in my arms.

I move one hand behind her head to stroke her hair. My fingers collide against the clip and I take it off. Her hair tumbles free.

I let my other hand fall to her waist to pull at the sash of her robe. The silk unravels.

Her hand climbs my thigh and gives it a squeeze. The sparks beneath her fingertips travel all the way to my crotch.

As I work on the buttons of her pajama top, her fingers crawl up my thigh. My cock rises to greet them.

"You seem to have grown better at removing buttons," Robyn observes after pulling away for a gasp of air.

I narrow my already half-lidded eyes at her. "You're not insinuating I've had practice, are you?"

I plant a kiss below her ear as I pop another button.

"Have you?"

I answer by cupping one of her breasts. Her engorged nipple pokes my palm and she inhales sharply.

"No fair," she accuses before pressing her palm against my crotch. It presses back against her skin with a quiver and my lips part.

I capture her mouth once more as I undo the last button and begin rubbing her nipples. Her shaking hand caresses me through the layers of fabric, and the inner one grows wet as I begin to leak.

I know she's leaking as well. I can smell the sweet scent in the air, sweeter than any of the flowers in the greenhouse. I'd slip my hand beneath her underwear and stroke her, but her stomach is in the way. I let out a groan into her mouth and settle for playing with her nipples. Then I nibble on an earlobe and suck on a patch of her neck.

Robyn's moans spill like a mist into the air. Each sound takes root beneath my skin and heat coils throughout my body like a merciless vine that strangles my senses.

I push her robe and her pajama top off her shoulders and playfully nip one before sinking to my knees on the ground in front of her. I pull her hips to the edge of the bench and wrench her pants and underwear off her. Her slippers fall off her feet.

I take a moment to stare at her. True, her body has changed. Her curves have grown. Apart from the obvious bump in the middle of her body, her breasts are fuller, her cheeks more rounded.

"See," Robyn says with a pout. "I've gotten fat."

"You're growing with the baby." I correct her. "So what? You're still as fascinating and as stunning as when I first met you."

Her brown eyes grow wide.

I plant a kiss on the valley between her breasts, then suckle on one of them. She moans. I do the same to the other, then press my lips reverently to her bloated tummy.

I feel something push against me in response and my own eyes widen.

"Did you feel that?" Robyn asks breathlessly.

I nod. I press my palm against her tummy again, and I feel that push again. I see a bubble form near the surface of her skin and my breath catches.

"Seems like your baby girl doesn't want me to kiss you," I say in awe.

Robyn grasps my chin. "Or maybe she's telling you to get on with in, Mr. Bolt."

"Demanding as her mother, huh?" I plant a lighter kiss on her tummy. "Well, I live to please."

I undo one final button, that of my pants, and pull the brass zipper down. I take my aching cock out of my boxers and move closer to the bench.

I grip her thighs and spread them before pushing up and in slowly. Robyn gasps.

I stop. "Are you okay?"

"Don't you dare stop."

I clench my jaw and narrow my eyes. "We better do something about that temper of yours."

I hold my breath as I push in the rest of way, then let it out as a low curse.

"Fuck."

She's tighter than ever, and the passage grips me even more as Robyn squeezes.

I meet her gaze and find her eyes half lidded, pupils dilated and eclipsed by lust that makes my own roar in my belly.

I take my cue and start moving inside her. Her stomach wobbles.

"I'm fine," Robyn assures me.

I nod and close my eyes. I couldn't stop even if I wanted to. There's no way to go but onwards. Harder. Faster. The protesting creaks of the bench travel throughout the greenhouse. Robyn's cries saturate the air.

My knees grind into the soil beneath me. My nails dig into her thighs as I bury myself deeper and deeper inside her.

As before, the heat is maddening, addictive.

Her wetness mingles with mine.

Suddenly, Robyn starts trembling. I open my eyes in time to see her mouth in an 'O'. Her eyelids squeeze shut and I see the hollow of her throat as she throws her head back. Her knuckles pale as her fingers grip the bench.

I manage a few more thrusts into the impossibly tight channel before succumbing to it. The pressure in my balls eases as I spill myself inside her, into her. Some of it trickles back down my cock.

I pull out and sit on the floor as my legs collapse. Robyn's legs, too, drop in front of me. Our panting breaks the silence above the muted breathing of the plants.

I fix myself up and zip my pants after getting on my feet. I wrap Robyn's robe back around her to keep her from getting cold.

As my fingers brush against her swollen stomach, I feel another kick and I smile.

I rub the stretched skin. "Not yet, little one."

The pressure fades.

I sit beside Robyn. "She's raring to get out."

"Yes," she agrees as she rubs her belly and looks down at it with unmistakable affection. "I can already tell she'll be as much a handful as the boys."

I nod. "She's more a warrior than a princess, so I guess the nursery doesn't suit her."

"She still needs a nursery, though," Robyn says. "How about we give that snobbish nursery a makeover? And by that, I mean we'll do all the work."

I glance at her. "You?"

"And you. We'll strip that room of all its pretenses."

And every touch of Caitlin, no doubt.

"Shouldn't you be resting?" I ask her.

"I think I should be more active, actually," Robyn answers. "And having a new hobby should do me some good. It'll help me take my mind off my fears."

"Okay," I give in. "Just let me do the hammering."

"And let you have all the fun?" She pouts. "I don't think so."

Chapter Twenty-One

Robyn

I drop the hammer into the box of tools beside my feet and let out a breath of relief. I wipe the sweat off my forehead as I stare at the painting hanging on the wall, a kitten sleeping soundly amid balls of yarn.

That's the last one.

My gaze travels across the room.

It's taken more than two weeks, sure, but now the nursery looks better than before.

All the pink wallpaper has been stripped off, leaving the walls bare and more soothing to the eyes. The carpet, too, has been discarded, though a fluffy, heart-shaped, cream-colored rug lies under the pink sleigh crib.

That I decided to keep, along with the shelves and the unicorn clock. The canopy is gone, though, and a mobile of stars hangs above the crib instead. The dolls on the shelf have been replaced by books. Colorful cat figurines stand in between them.

In lieu of the carousel lamp that gave me the creeps, a pair of lamps with stained glass shades spill light into the room. A cozy rocking chair has taken the place of the ridiculous throne.

Apart from the paintings of baby animals in handmade wooden frames, I've also added some fresh plants which Linda picked and a small indoor fountain to make the room more calming.

I place my hand on my tummy. "Now, that's much better, isn't it?"

The baby kicks in response and I smile.

"You're right," a voice agrees from behind me. "It is more fit for a baby now."

I turn and smile at Geoffrey. "No interior decorator was needed, after all."

"Maybe you should be one." Geoffrey touches his chin. "I can sense your passion and your talent."

I shake my head. "Once the baby is out, I'm going to have my hands full."

"Right." He nods. "I never did get to take care of a baby since Jillian was already almost three when we got her, but I've heard horror stories."

My eyebrows perk up.

"Don't be scared, though." Geoffrey grabs my hand. "We're all here for you. Xander has asked all of us to help you should you need it."

My eyebrows furrow. "He did?"

Geoffrey squeezes my hand. "I didn't think he was serious about you at first, but he cares so much about you."

I have noticed that Xander's become even more protective now. He constantly asks how I'm feeling.

"And why shouldn't he?" Geoffrey goes on. "He'd be a fool to not see how good you are for him."

I point a finger at my chest. "You think I'm good for him?"

"My dear girl, don't you see? He's changed completely because of you."

Really?

"You've given him a purpose, and that is all a person needs to be better and live fully."

Now I'm even more puzzled.

He pats my shoulder. "Well, even if Xander didn't ask, we'd still help you. We are your..."

"Family," I finish the sentence.

Of course, I haven't forgotten that this is all playing house, and I'm still afraid that Geoffrey and Linda and Jillian might find out the truth and hate me. I'm still afraid that the past is going to catch up to me and swallow all of us up. But with each day, my fears of the past grow dimmer in comparison to my hopes for the future.

I place a hand on my stomach. Geoffrey squeezes my shoulder.

"Have you thought of a name yet?" he asks.

I shrug. "Xander and I were thinking about naming her after my mother or his, but then we decided she should have a name of her own. We just haven't thought of one yet."

"Well, you still have three months, don't you?"

I nod.

Geoffrey steps under the skylight and looks up at the heavens. "Time flies so fast, though. Why, it seems only yesterday that summer began, and now it's ending. Autumn will be upon us soon. Why, some leaves have already started to fall."

As if on cue, a leaf touches the glass before riding away on the tide of the breeze.

Geoffrey turns to me. "Autumn is my favorite season. Everything is at its most beautiful just before dying or disappearing, you know. Like fireworks."

I understand.

Autumn is my favorite season, too. There are leaves to kick. There's a certain crispness to the air. And it was my Dad's favorite, too. After all, he and Wesley...

My train of thought skids to a halt. My hand rises to press against my lips.

"Is something wrong?" Geoffrey asks.

I glance at the calendar on the wall. "I just remembered that my Dad and my brother's birthdays are coming up soon."

I've been so busy with, well, being married and pregnant, that I nearly forgot about it.

I didn't, though.

I approach the calendar on the wall and flip the top page to look at the next.

"Any plans?" Geoffrey asks.

I put my finger on the twelfth. "I was hoping I could do the same thing I did last year."

~

"...and the year before that," I say to Xander as I sit in front of my dresser with my comb in my hands.

My thumb runs over the teeth.

He pauses in the act of drying his hair. "What is that, exactly?"

"Just visit their graves," I tell him. "I only visit once a year, on their birthdays. My Mom's was in February, but Wesley and Dad share theirs in September. I don't visit on the anniversary of their deaths because, well..." I continue combing my hair "...it's just too sad."

"And that's in California?" Xander asks.

I nod.

Xander draws a deep breath. "Can't you just skip it this year because you're pregnant?"

"No," I answer quickly. "That's no excuse. Dr. Strafford says everything is fine with me and it's okay for me to travel. And it's not like I'm going to travel to the other end of the world."

He folds his arms over his bare chest. "And what if Howie is there waiting for you, hmm?"

"Why would he be? He doesn't know about my family."

All I ever told him about them was that they were gone.

Xander falls silent. His brows furrow in contemplation.

I go over to him and touch his arm. "Xander, I have to go. I know I have a new family now, but I don't want to forget the one I had. If I do, who will remember them?"

Still, he says nothing.

"I miss them now more than ever," I add.

Xander scratches his nape and sighs. "Fine. We'll go visit their graves."

"We?" My eyebrows shoot up.

"What? You think I'd let you go alone?" He takes the towel off his shoulders and wraps it around mine. "If you're going to visit them then I'm coming with you. I am your husband, after all."

So he frequently reminds me.

I smile and touch his cheek. "Thank you. I'm sure they'd love to meet you, too."

~

I let my knees fall on the carpet of leaves on the ground. A soft breeze rustles some of them and the strands of hair flowing from my red bonnet.

I take off my mitten and run my fingers over the names of my father, mother and brother carved into the slab of cold stone. I blow them a kiss before setting down the bouquet of flowers in my arm and the jar of apricot jam in my other hand.

The jam both Dad and Wesley loved so much that they sometimes fought over it.

"What happens to the jam?" Xander asks behind me.

I shrug. "I don't know. Does it matter, though?"

I stand up and join Xander's side. I grab his arm but my eyes remain on the tombstone.

"Mom, Dad, Wes, this is my husband, Xander. He's a good man, so don't haunt him."

I touch my belly.

"Oh, and I'm pregnant, too, with a baby girl. I hope you'll watch over her."

Of course I don't hear an answer. I never do. It would be beyond spooky if I did. Still, talking to them eases the burden on my chest.

I squeeze Xander's arm. "You say something, too."

He clears his throat. "Noah, Jacqueline, Wesley, you can rest in peace. I promise I'll..."

He stops suddenly.

I turn to him and find his eyes wide. His cheeks look a tad pale.

"What's wrong, Xander?" I ask him curiously.

His eyes remain glued to the tombstone. "Your family, they all died on Christmas Eve six years ago?"

Right. I never told him the details.

"They were at a Christmas party at a friend's apartment," I explain. "I was supposed to be there, too, but I fell asleep at the hotel. By the time I woke up, the fire was all over the news."

"The fire?"

"I tried calling Wesley, since he said he wasn't going to go to the party, but as it turns out, he stopped by there, too, since his friend had other plans." I purse my lips and draw a deep breath. "None of them made it out of the burning building alive. Not many people did."

Xander falls silent. Now his whole face looks pale.

"Xander?"

"I'm sorry." He shrugs my hand off his arm and steps away from me. "I just... I... I'll be back."

Without a coherent explanation, he walks off.

My eyebrows furrow.

That's weird. He's never acted like that before. Did I say something wrong? Or did I perhaps remind him of something painful from his own past?

I'm tempted to run after him, but I don't.

I turn my gaze back to the tombstone and draw a deep breath.

Oh well. Whatever it is, I'll just talk to him la—

"Hello, Robyn."

The voice stops my heart and sends shivers up my spine. The hairs on the back of my neck stand up.

Slowly, I lift my head, and my stomach coils when my eyes clash with those dark blue ones. I freeze.

No.

"What's the matter? Did you think you'd never see me again?"

Howie comes closer. The dried leaves crackle beneath his boots. With each step he takes, the blood drains from my body. Fear creeps beneath my skin.

"Surely you didn't think I'd just let you go after..."

He stops as he comes around the tombstone, his eyes on my stomach. His jaw clenches and his nostrils flare.

I manage to step back, but I still can't find my voice.

No.

"You're... pregnant?"

Howie's eyebrows crease and his hand rolls into a fist. I hear the crack of a knuckle.

He steps forward. "Why, you..."

Chapter Twenty-Two

Xander

I catch the man's fist squarely in my palm as I step between him and Robyn.

His midnight blue eyes grow wide and I narrow mine. My jaw clenches.

"Robyn, step back," I instruct her through gritted teeth.

I hear the rustle of leaves beneath her shoes as she shuffles her feet.

The midnight blue eyes in front of me narrow as well, adding to the creases on his forehead. I feel the tension coiling in his knuckles, and my other hand rolls into a fist, ready to retaliate.

Adrenaline pumps through my veins.

Suddenly, though, his fist relaxes and he withdraws. His shoulders rise and fall as he takes a deep breath with his teeth buried into his lower lip. His gaze falls to the ground and then scours me from my feet to the top of my head.

I do the same.

This man is shorter than me, maybe 5'8" at best, and his build is smaller than mine, too, but I can sense a tenacity that his physique fails to manifest. The toned muscles suggest athleticism, the scars experience in close combat, and the multiple tattoos a bad attitude—although the one of his name right across his neck simply shouts narcissism.

Howie Mitchell.

"Who are you?" he asks as he sticks out his chin.

I stick my chest out and cross my arms over it. "Xander Bolt. Robyn's husband."

He spits on the ground. "That can't be true."

I show him the gold band on my finger.

His gaze narrows again. "And you've knocked her up, I see. Tell me, did she squeal like a pig?"

My fist clenches. My muscles tense as they prepare for battle.

"Did she squeeze you like a vise just like I taught her to do?"

Anger rises up to my throat and forms a knot. My nape prickles and I can hear my upper teeth grinding against the lower.

There's nothing I want more than to beat this scumbag to a pulp and feed his half-dead carcass to a swarm of sharks, or maybe hang him from a tree and let vultures pick the flesh off his bones as he endures a slow death. I force myself to calm down, though, knowing I am the more civilized of savage beasts here.

I can't fight him. Not here. Not now, with Robyn watching and her safety not guaranteed.

One day, maybe, but not today.

Unfortunately.

"Leave," I order him.

Howie shakes his head.

"I don't know how many men you have with you, but I can assure you that twice that number of cops are on their way this minute. I sent them a message as soon as I spotted you."

Howie snorts. "You married a cop, Robyn?" He clicks his tongue. "I'm disappointed."

"Good," I say instead of bothering to correct him. "Because she was never made to please you."

His nostrils flare.

I raise my chin. "Leave, or stay and get arrested. Either way is fine with me."

He says nothing, nor does he show any sign of leaving.

His hand goes to his pocket and I shift my feet, bracing myself to disarm him if he pulls a gun.

Then his phone rings.

I watch him take it out of his pocket and tap the screen before holding it to his ear.

"Yes?" He answers the call without taking his eyes off me.

I don't take my eyes off him, either.

I have no idea who he's talking to, but he doesn't say anything more. He just grunts and hangs up. His hand drops to his side.

"It seems I have to leave for now." His gaze goes past me to Robyn.

"No," I tell him. "You're going to leave Robyn alone for good, because the next time I see you will be the last."

He shrugs. "Maybe. Maybe I'll kill you in front of Robyn, since she seems to care for you."

I hear Robyn gasp.

I open my mouth to say more, but he turns his back on me and starts running. I hold my breath until he's out of sight. Even then, I don't let my guard down until I hear the wailing of sirens.

Only then do I let out a sigh of relief, though that vanishes when I hear a rustle behind me.

I turn to see Robyn kneeling on the ground. Her shoulders are shuddering and her shaking hands are clasped to her chest as if in prayer. Her pale, parted lips quiver. Her gaze bores a hole into the earth.

"Robyn."

I kneel in front of her just as she buries her face in her hands and breaks into sobs. I mutter a curse under my breath and pull her against my chest, which grows tight as the embers of my anger flame into a fierce hatred for the man who just did this to her.

That fucking piece of shit.

"It's alright," I assure her in the calmest voice I can manage as I press my mouth to her forehead and stroke her hair. "You've got me. And I'm not going to let that bastard come within a mile of you again."

~

"Ty, tell me you've got something on Howard Mitchell," I say as soon as Tyrone picks up the phone.

"What did he do before my pals got there?" Tyrone throws a question back at me.

"Nothing." I stop pacing the balcony and sink into an armchair. "Except scare the hell out of my wife."

She didn't say a word all throughout the trip home, not on the plane or in the car. She didn't eat anything either, contenting herself with sips from a bottle of water. And when we got home, she went straight to the bedroom. The last time I peeked in, she was huddled under the blanket, still shaking.

"Did he threaten to hurt her?" Tyrone asks.

"Oh, he threatened a lot of things," I answer, my blood boiling just to remember them.

"Then maybe a lawyer could build a case on that. You know a good one, don't you?"

"Yes," I answer as I recall my earlier conversation with Matt. "And I've already asked him to file for a restraining order against Howard Mitchell. But that's not enough. I need Howie put away. I don't need a case. I need evidence."

"Sorry," Ty says. "But he's not in the system. If the guy is the psycho you're saying he is, he's a psycho who knows how to cover his tracks."

I shake my head. He may be smart, smart enough to know Robyn wouldn't be able to resist visiting her family's graves. But he's not that smart.

"I'll send you a file," I tell Ty. "It's a scan of a sketch I made of the bastard."

"You sketched the guy?"

On the plane.

"I didn't even know you still sketched."

"I want you to pay special attention to his tattoos," I continue. "I'm sure they'll be in some database somewhere."

"Okay. I'll do my best. I don't want to let you down."

"Never mind letting me down," I tell him. "Just keep my wife safe."

"If he comes near her again, call the cops."

"If he comes near her again, I might not be able to stop myself from breaking his neck. So find a way to make sure he doesn't."

Tyrone exhales. "Well, there's a bit of the old Xander I used to adore."

I ignore the remark.

"Get me something," I tell him. "Please."

"I won't stop until I do," he promises.

I let out a sigh of relief. "Thank you, Ty."

"Take care, Xander."

He hangs up and I hunch over my laptop to send him the file I promised. Afterwards, I sit back and rub my temples.

I knew Howie was a despicable freak, but I didn't think he'd be calculatingly insane. He's dangerous, and he wants Robyn back, maybe more than anything.

I better make sure that doesn't happen.

I sigh, this time in exhaustion.

Howie, however, isn't my only problem.

There's also the fact that Robyn's parents and her brother all died in a fire on Christmas Eve six years ago.

It can't be a coincidence.

Just a cruel trick of fate.

I run my hands through my hair in frustration. My nails dig into my scalp.

How the hell did everything fall apart so fast?

Chapter Twenty-Three

Robyn

I can't let myself fall apart.

I tell myself that as I mix some vanilla into a pot of heated cream, milk, sugar and gelatin on the kitchen counter.

Sure, I've just found out that Howie is still obsessed with me and will do anything to get me back. Sure, he hates the baby even if it's his own. And yes, I'm feeling more drained than ever. Every part of my body is sore and aching and seemingly taking on a life of its own. The tears keep coming—and they're not the only fluids my body seems too keen on getting rid of—and my chest feels combustible, the heartburn never-ending. Oh, and there's the fact that none, absolutely none, of my former clothes fit anymore and those that do don't look flattering in the least. I've never been a vain person, but I swear I've never felt more unattractive in my life.

I'm losing my shit.

Even so, I can't fall apart. My baby is counting on me.

I glance at my tummy, more bloated than ever, and my lips curve into a soft smile.

I'm a mother. I have to be strong. Stronger than I've ever been.

Besides, Xander said he'd keep me safe. It's probably why he seems to be so busy lately.

I've seen less of him, but I have to trust him.

I have to get my shit together.

"There she is," Jillian says as she walks into the kitchen in a denim jacket over a red blouse and jeans. "My favorite cousin-in-law."

I arch my eyebrows at her. "Aren't I your only cousin-in-law?"

"Well, Matt has a few cousins, but I don't know them well." She leans on the counter. "What are you making?"

"Panna cotta," I answer.

She dips her finger into the mixture and slips it between her lips. "Mmm. It tastes good already."

I slowly pour the mixture into the glasses I've prepared.

"I'm glad to see you here in the kitchen making something," Jillian says as she watches me. "I thought you'd be sulking over your crazy ex."

Well, I was.

I narrow my eyes at her. "You've heard about my ex?"

"Of course I have. Xander did call Matt about a restraining order, you know."

I didn't know about that.

"I guess that's another thing you and Xander have in common, huh? Nasty exes that can't let you go."

"Unfortunately."

I scoop the remaining mixture into the last glass.

"Is he as bad as Matt said he was?"

"Worse," I answer without the bat of an eyelash.

Jillian taps her French manicured fingers on the counter. "I see."

I set the empty pot down in the sink.

"Well, don't worry about it. You belong to Xander, and Xander doesn't let anyone take his stuff away."

Ah. So I'm property, am I?

"He won't let anyone hurt you," Jillian goes on. "I'm sure of it. And he's not the only one."

She places her hand on my shoulder.

"Matt and I are here, and Linda and Geoffrey. You're not alone. We're all in this together."

That's what I feared, though. What if Howie tries to hurt them to get to me? I wouldn't put that past him.

"Thanks." I turn around to face her. "But this is my mess."

"Oh, stop it." Jillian runs her fingers through my hair. "You've got enough messes to worry about, don't you?

And trust me, you'll have many more. You'll need all the help you can get."

I don't answer.

"Speaking of mess makers, how is our little princess?" Jillian puts a hand on my tummy.

"She seems perfectly fine," I reply.

"And you?"

"I feel like an elephant."

Jillian laughs. "Well, so did I. I still don't know how I fit those boys in here."

She touches her own tummy.

"One question." She puts her arm around me. "Do you guys still do it?"

"Do what?" I raise my eyebrows.

"Sex, of course."

I blush.

The last time we had sex was at the greenhouse. After that, we got busy with fixing up the nursery, which drained all of my energy. Then we went to California and then Howie showed up. And lately, he doesn't seem to be in the mood, though I can't say the same for myself.

"Are you getting any?" Jillian asks.

"I'm fine," I tell her. "That's the least of my concerns."

She pouts. "Well, I'm only asking because there were times that I was super horny during my pregnancy, even during the third trimester, and I had to beg Matt to give me some. Some people think it's weird, but hey, the whole pregnancy thing is weird. And don't even think it will hurt the baby. It won't. You have needs, too, and that's fine."

I look at her. "I didn't say anything."

And frankly, this topic is getting uncomfortable.

I head back to the counter. "Help me put these in the fridge, will you?"

"Sure."

I grab one glass and open the fridge. She grabs the rest two at a time and puts them in.

"Thanks." I close the door of the refrigerator.

Jillian gasps.

I throw her a puzzled look. "What is it?"

"I just got this perfect idea to cheer you up," she says.

"And?"

"A baby shower!" She grabs my hands. "You haven't had one, have you?"

"No."

"I'll throw one for you." She touches her forehead. "Oh, I don't know why I didn't think of this earlier. I can't believe I almost forgot all about it."

"You don't have to, Jill."

But she's not listening. As she taps a finger on her chin, I can tell the wheels in her head are already turning. Fast.

"I have to make the preparations right away."

She walks off but stops after a few steps to turn and give me a wide smile.

"Don't you worry. I'm going to throw you the sweetest, bubbliest, most sensational baby shower ever."

~

Jillian wasn't kidding.

From the steps of the patio, I can see the literal bubbles dancing on the breeze, the constant stream blown by not just one but four bubble machines. I can see the pastries on a long table—cupcakes with rainbow sprinkles, sugar-coated cookies, fudge-topped brownies, pastel-colored macaroons, éclairs, profiteroles, tarts and donuts. A chocolate fountain sits on another table and a bar serves milkshakes. Bar tables have been set up draped in rainbow-colored linen. Colorful balloons and fresh flower arrangements are everywhere, too.

The most eye-catching piece, though, is the cake with colorful layers decked with sleeping baby animals—a chick, an elephant calf, a panda cub, a puppy, a kitten.

On the topmost layer sits a sleeping baby girl with red hair looking snug under a pink blanket.

I smile.

"Like it?" Jillian asks as she climbs up the steps.

"You outdid yourself," I tell her. "Again."

"Well, I had lots of fun arranging it," she admits as she gazes at the garden. Then she lets out a sigh. "It made me wish even more for a baby girl."

I place my hand on her shoulder. "I'm sure you'll have one of your own."

She nods. "Oh well, this isn't about me. It's about you, so I hope you'll have fun."

"I'm already having fun," I say as I look around. "I don't see Xander, though."

"Oh, he'll be here soon." Jillian grabs my hand and gives it a squeeze before leading me down the stairs. "Come."

She introduces me to the guests, all of whom she seems to know and many of whom I've already met at my wedding. The only additions are her friends from Austin and Maverick's schools as well as Dr. Stafford.

"You look well." Dr. Stafford casts an admiring smile at the chartreuse dress beneath my white shawl.

"Thank you." I smile back. "And thank you for coming."

"Well, Mrs. Barrett was rather insistent."

I chuckle. "That she can be."

"And well, this isn't so bad." She looks around. "I especially love the linens and the flowers."

"They'd fit right in your waiting room."

She chuckles. "Right you are. But don't worry. I won't steal a thing, maybe just an idea."

I grin. "Well, those are free."

She nods and moves along. I head to the pastry table to grab a profiterole and I've just put in my mouth when another woman approaches.

"Congratulations," the woman in a cream-colored blouse and jeans felicitates as she grabs a macaroon.

"Thank you," I tell her.

I don't recognize her, so she must be another of Jillian's friends from school.

"Having a baby is by no means easy," she goes on after stuffing the macaroon inside her mouth. "And I'm not just talking about the actual birth, which is a literal pain in the ass and other parts..."

I try not to grimace at that.

"..but the whole baby thing. But hey, try to look on the bright side, okay?" She pats my arm. "They grow too fast."

She glances at a group of children chasing bubbles.

"I'll keep that in mind," I tell her.

She rubs her bare arms. "It's a chilly day, isn't it? It's a good thing you have these patio heaters around."

I glance at one of them. Jillian thought of everything, of course.

"I'd love to use one, but I'm scared they might start a fire."

I didn't think of that.

"But of course you're not." She smiles at me. "After all, you're married to a fireman."

Chapter Twenty-Four

Xander

"You were a fireman?" Robyn asks me at the patio after the party.

I nearly choke on my cup of coffee.

I set it down on the table beside me. "Who told you that?"

She sits on the wicker chair on the other side of the table.

"Someone at the party."

I frown. I shouldn't have let Jillian invite whoever she wanted.

No. I should have been at the party from the start.

I let Robyn out of my sight for a moment and this is what happens.

I grit my teeth as I grab my cup of coffee and hold it tight between my palms.

I was keeping my distance from her, worried about what she might do if she found out the truth. And of course that's exactly why she found out.

Or has she?

"What were you told, exactly?" I ask as I lift the cup to my lips.

Robyn shrugs. "Just that you used to be a fireman."

So she doesn't know.

I let out a breath of relief.

"I used to be," I confess. "But it wasn't a long stint."

"Was that the job you were talking about? The one you lost because of Tracy?"

"No," I lie. "That was different. That was for a graphic design firm."

"Oh."

"I was the one who quit being a firefighter."

That's true.

"Because?" Robyn leans closer to me.

"Because it was too tough."

Not a lie.

"Okay." Robyn sits back in her chair and lets out a sigh. "I wish you had told me, though. I hate finding out your secrets from others."

"It wasn't a secret."

"But you didn't tell me about it." She sighs again. "I realize there's still so much I don't know about you. And given the circumstances of our marriage I know I don't have the right to ask you about anything, but I still wish I knew the person I sleep with every night."

I set down my cup. "Yeah. Sometimes, I wish I knew more about you, too."

Her eyebrows arch. "Like?"

"You haven't exactly told me everything about Howie," I tell her.

Robyn frowns. "I don't want to remember that."

"I understand." I lean forward on my knees. "I'm not going to ask you to relive all that. I'd like to know more about him, though."

"Why?"

"So I know who I'm up against."

Robyn's eyebrows furrow as she sits up. "You're going after him?"

"I'm making sure he never bothers you again," I answer as I look into her eyes. "Which is what I promised you."

She sits back and succumbs to a bout of silence.

I pick up my cup again and drink as I wait for her to break it.

"It's embarrassing to say this, but I don't really know him," Robyn says, her gaze on the distant horizon. "We met at a party like I told you. We got drunk. We kissed.

We had sex. Repeat. And before I knew it, he was my boyfriend."

I push the image of her and Howie out of my mind and wash down the bitter taste of jealousy with another mouthful of coffee.

"What can you tell me about him? And I mean facts, not descriptions. I can come up with enough adjectives to describe him myself."

Twisted. Sadistic. Arrogant.

"He was in this gang called Hips."

"Hips?" I raise my eyebrow.

"That's just what they called themselves. Don't ask me why. He was just an underling before, but everybody respected him and he was definitely on his way up. He's the leader now, I think. The old one must be dead or in jail. Also, now, they seem to be working with some Russian mob."

My eyebrows go up again. "Russian mob."

Robyn touches her chin. "Yeah, but wait, I don't think they're officially affiliated yet. They're still trying to prove their worth, I think."

"How many men does he have in his gang?" I ask.

"Not many," she answers. "Less than twenty, I believe. But he has these three faithful lackeys that he keeps with him at all times. Very dangerous men, maybe even more so than him in some respects. I'm surprised we didn't see them at the cemetery."

I frown. "What can you tell me about them?"

"Their names are Vaughn, Tom and Ian. At least, that's what Howie calls them. Ian is the oldest. Forties. When he curses, he sounds like an Irishman. Vaughn is the biggest. He whittles and he's as sadistic as Howie. Tom is the smartest. He's got a bunch of thorny vines tattooed to his back."

I commit the details to memory.

"Ian used to be a Marine, I think. He can punch. Vaughn likes hunting. I think he lived in Africa for a bit. Worked as some kind of bodyguard. Tom was in jail once."

I throw Robyn a puzzled look. "You're right, those guys do sound scarier than Howie. So how come they follow him?"

"There's something about Howie that inspires—no, commands—respect. And if you don't give it to him, he'll beat the hell out of you."

"He can beat the hell out of those three guys?"

"I saw him do it to Vaughn once."

Hearing that makes me glad I didn't tangle with him at the cemetery. He might have taken me apart and then taken Robyn away forever.

"Plus he's clever," Robyn adds. "Cleverer than Tom when he puts his brains to use."

"You mean when he's sober."

She nods. "Yeah, I guess. Those three, they're bad. But Howie? He's evil."

I sensed that, too.

I finish my coffee in one final gulp and set the empty cup down.

"Any idea how he turned out that way?" I ask.

To my surprise, Robyn reaches across to wipe a drop of coffee from the corner of my mouth with her thumb. Even more surprising, she slips that thumb past her lips.

My breath catches.

"I miss coffee."

I still the throbbing of my heart, and of something else that's suddenly alert, and steer the conversation back on track.

"So, any ideas?"

She places her hands on her lap. "You're asking me to read the mind of a lunatic?"

"Well, you know him better than anyone."

She glares at me.

Shit. I shouldn't have said that.

"Just give me an idea."

Her eyebrows crease as she looks away. "I think it has something to do with his stepmother. She was crazy, too, I think."

That makes sense. People don't usually drive themselves mad. They give what they get. They become what they're made.

"I think he might have killed her," Robyn adds.

Not shocking.

"Anything else about him?"

"He likes nature. That's one reason why he has a house in the middle of the woods. I think he has a house by a lake, too, somewhere in Wisconsin."

I take note of that.

"Well, he says he has those houses because he likes nature, but I think it's because they're remote and he can do whatever he wants in them."

My shoulders tense.

Robyn turns to me. "Can we just stop talking about him now?" She shakes her head. "I don't think I can do this anymore."

"Sure," I say. "Thanks for everything you've told me."

She nods, her gaze back on something distant.

"And I'm sorry. I won't ask about him again. It's time we put the past behind us and prepare for the future."

"The future," Robyn repeats as she glances down at her tummy and puts a hand on it.

I put my hand on top of hers and she smiles.

"You're right. Isn't that why Jillian threw this baby shower for us? To remind us of what the future can bring?"

I scratch my head. "Is that why she did it?"

"We can't keep looking back at the past or it'll catch up to us," Robyn says. "Worse, we'll lose sight of what's going on now and what's ahead."

I squeeze her hand.

She's right. We may not be able to shrug off the past, but we can stop dwelling on it and move on.

We can't let the past catch up to us.

~

Smoke.

Fire.

The sound of screams and the smell of burning flesh.

No!

I wake up with a jolt. Beads of sweat trickle down the sides of my face. My heart hammers inside my bare chest, which rises and falls in turn as I gasp for air.

I slap my moist forehead.

That nightmare. Again.

And just when I thought I'd never have it anymore, when I've made up my mind to put the past behind me.

No. It's just a dream. Just a dream.

I mustn't dwell on it.

I close my eyes and wait for my heartbeat to slow down. Then I shake off the cobwebs of my nightmare and get off the bed.

My gaze falls on it and my eyes grow wide as I realize it's empty. Only a pile of pillows occupies the opposite side.

Robyn's not here?

Panic seizes me and I rush off without grabbing my robe. As I enter the walk-in closet, I hear sounds from the bathroom and I breathe a sigh of relief.

Good. She's safe.

My relief turns into something else, though, as I approach the bathroom door and realize exactly what the sounds are.

Whimpers. Moans.

Cries of pleasure that go straight to my cock and send a shiver up my spine. A knot forms in my throat.

I swallow it as I slowly push the bathroom door open. My eyes grow wide as they rest on Robyn's naked body perched on the toilet, her knees spread and her back against the tank. Her eyes are squeezed shut and her lips are parted. One of her hands is rubbing a nipple and the other is resting between her legs.

No. Not resting. Stroking.

The sight of it sends my cock pulsing and straining against my boxers. My balls swell and fresh beads of sweat break out on my skin as my heart starts pounding anew.

"Fuck."

Chapter Twenty-Five

Robyn

Shit.

My eyes fly open to clash with green-gold ones peering through the bathroom door. My hands freeze. Fresh bubbles of heat burst in my cheeks.

"Xa—Xander?"

He enters the room and sits on his heels on the rug. His eyes stare right between my legs.

"Continue."

The crisp order—not a request—sends fresh sparks of excitement through my veins. I hesitate for a second. For one thing, I've never done this in front of someone of my own free will before and I feel embarrassed. But I have done it, when Howie forced me to, and unpleasant memories suddenly fill my mind. But the raw lust in Xander's eyes—not a desire to humiliate, only primal lust without any ulterior motives—stokes the fire already raging in my belly. My unfulfilled desire takes over and I close my eyes as I continue to tease my stiff nipple and rub the swollen bud of flesh between my legs.

I shiver.

Even with my eyes closed, I can feel Xander's scorching gaze on my hands, on my nipples, on the dripping, wide-open crack between my trembling legs. I can hear the sploshes mixed in with my moans.

I'm close. So close.

In the past, when Howie watched me, I always tried to hold myself back. I didn't want to enjoy myself because I didn't want him to enjoy the show. Because that would only mean my defeat, my shame.

But now, I feel like I'm the victor here and I feel no shame. I revel in the sensations coursing beneath my skin, in the excitement of being watched so intently.

I half open my eyes to meet Xander's as my hips jerk. My body quakes as the drenched hand between my legs grows still. A cry spills past my lips.

Then I lie back against the toilet, breathless and tired.

But not entirely exhausted or satisfied.

Jill's right. Pregnancy can make you feel super horny. It doesn't matter how big you are or how much of a mess you are. You still want to get some.

No. I want to get a lot.

Xander stands up and offers me his hand, and I grab it and throw myself into his arms. I grip his shoulders and capture his mouth with mine. His hands cup my face as his tongue slips past my lips.

Without pulling away, he leads me out of the bathroom and towards the bed. We collapse on top of it and he turns me on my side. He tugs at my earlobe with his teeth as his fingers find my sensitive nipple.

I cry out and clutch the sheets.

He kisses my neck as his hand slips between my legs. His fingers brush against my tingling nub before sliding inside me without any resistance.

I shiver. My mouth presses against the back of my free hand which muffles my next cry.

As his fingers move in and out, my hips begin to move on their own. His other hand crawls beneath me to toy with my nipple.

My eyes grow moist. The back of my hand grows moist.

And the place between my legs grows wetter.

But I'm not the only one who's wet.

I can feel the beads of sweat against my back. I can feel the leaking tip of his cock behind me.

I try to reach for it but fail.

He strokes me faster and I grip the sheets with both hands. My mouth gapes open to let out an even louder cry as a wave of exquisite pleasure sweeps over me once more.

I shudder in the aftermath, gasping for air.

Xander's hands leave me. When I glance over my shoulder, I find him standing by the bed, that predatory gaze still in his eyes. His boxers pile around his ankles.

He kicks them away but before he can climb onto the bed, I kneel in front of him and take his cock inside my mouth.

He lets out a gasp and then a grunt as he clutches my shoulders with trembling hands. One of his hands goes up to my hair and his fingers join the tangle there.

I grip his hips and move my head back and forth. His cock glides across my tongue and I taste something both bitter and salty.

Then Xander pushes me away and pulls me to my feet. He throws me on the bed, back on my side, lies down behind me and enters me.

Again, I grip the sheets. Again, I scream.

His fingers bite my hips and they rock with his as he thrusts deep inside me. My vision blurs with my thoughts.

His fingers find my nub of flesh, and within moments I'm unraveling again. Breath leaves my lungs. The explosion of my orgasm travels all the way to my curled toes.

Xander continues his thrusts as I lie limp. The bed shakes.

I'm not done yet.

When I've recovered some of my strength, I pull away from Xander and push him down on the bed. I straddle him, facing away from him, and lower myself on his cock. I start moving my hips.

He does the same. His cock slides in and out of me as I bounce on top of him.

I can feel my stomach wobbling and my breasts jiggling. My hair bounces off my shoulders.

I stop moving, but Xander doesn't. His hand clings to my hips as he pounds into me. The other reaches for my breast.

He moves faster. The sound of skin slapping against skin fills the room, along with the smell of sweat and sex.

Heat swirls within me anew.

With a groan as loud as my cry, he pulls me down on him at the same time that pleasure seizes me. His cock quivers and spurts inside me as I tremble. I lean back and grip his arms.

Unable to support my weight, I fall on top of him as strength leaves my arms. Now, I have none left. The embers of my desire have gone out, too, though I've lost count of how many orgasms it took to extinguish them.

"Who would have thought a pregnant woman would have so much libido?"

"My thoughts exactly," Xander says in my ear, making me realize that I've just spoken out loud.

He wraps his arms around me and nuzzles my neck.

"But I can't say I don't like it."

I grin.

"You better not look forward to more, though," I warn him. "I think I've just used up all the energy I've built up so far, and I have to save some for childbirth."

He frowns against my cheek.

"Well, at least I was able to join you." He kisses my cheek. "Why didn't you invite me in the first place?"

I glance at him. "You've been busy lately. And deep in thought."

"Sorry."

I kiss him. "Don't worry too much, okay? I'm the one giving birth, you know."

"I know." He places a hand over my belly. "And that's not what I was worried about."

"I know." I stare at the ceiling as I place my hand over his. "But we've just decided to put the past behind us, right? It's time to put it away to make room for new memories."

~

New and better memories, I think to myself as I go through the pictures that the photographer took of the baby shower. My favorite shows me and Xander smiling beside the tall cake.

I smile as I run my fingers over the glossy photo.

Then I have an idea.

I decide to frame some and hang them on the nursery wall. There's still room, after all. And if I remember correctly, there were a few spare handmade picture frames.

The question is: Where are they?

I look for Xander to ask him, but I can't seem to find him around the house. He must be in the gym by the pool, or maybe he went out.

I consider calling him but decide against it. I'll just look for the frames myself.

I head to the storage room opposite the den in the basement. It isn't locked, so I simply push the door open. That sends the sheets of dust swirling into the air, and I place my hand on my belly as I let out a sneeze.

I better make this quick.

My gaze goes over the boxes as I search for the frames. My lips curve into a grin as I catch a glimpse of a frame sticking out of one of them.

"Aha!"

I approach the box and open it. My smile turns upside down as I realize my mistake.

This frame isn't like the ones in the nursery.

Still, I turn it around. A gasp escapes my lips as I stare at an image of Xander in his firefighter's uniform. The bulky black suit with the yellow reflective tape looks mighty fine on him. My heart skips a beat.

Then it stops as I take a closer look at the picture and see the logo on the uniform.

SFFD.

San Francisco?

But that's where...

My thoughts stop in their tracks, too, as I see what's lying beneath the framed picture—a pile of newspaper clippings, the topmost one about the fire on Christmas Eve six years ago.

The same fire where my parents and Wesley died.

I go through the other clippings and they're all about the same thing.

The Fir-Nace, some newspapers called the tragedy, because it was reportedly started by a Christmas tree that caught fire.

I drop to the dust-covered floor as my breath leaves me. My mouth gapes as my eyes stare blankly ahead. My mind spins as it connects the dots.

Xander being a firefighter in San Francisco, where my parents died. Xander not wanting to talk about it.

The missed phone call. The unforgiveable mistake. Tracy saying she saved his life. That serious look in his eyes when he says he knows he can't save everyone.

I clamp a hand over my mouth as I gasp. Tears sting my eyes.

It can't be.

And yet I have a feeling it is.

I have to know for sure.

~

"Were you or were you not one of the firefighters who responded to that burning building in San Francisco six years ago on Christmas Eve?" I ask Xander with a trembling voice as soon as he walks into the bedroom. "That burning building where my mom, my dad and Wesley died?"

He throws me a puzzled look.

I toss the newspaper clippings at his feet.

Xander kneels on the floor and picks them up. "Where did you get these?"

"Answer my question," I insist. "Were you?"

Xander draws a deep breath.

"Were you?"

"All of the units in the city were asked to respond to that fire," he finally answers.

"Including yours?"

"Mine was one of the first. That fire was primarily in our jurisdiction."

A lump forms in my throat.

"But I didn't get the call until it was too late."

"Because of Tracy," I whisper as I sink onto the edge of the bed.

"Because I was reckless," he corrects me. "I wasn't as responsible as I should have been."

He steps forward.

"When I got there, the fire was already out of control, but I knew there were still a lot of people trapped inside. I could hear them screaming."

I place a hand over my heart as my chest tightens. Fresh tears brim in my eyes.

"My captain ordered me to stay out, but I tried to get inside anyway. Before I could, the building collapsed."

I slide to the floor. A teardrop falls on the carpet.

"A lot of my friends died that night. I should have died with them. I should have been there sooner and saved some lives."

My chest begins to heave. "You could have saved them."

"Yes. I was the best they had."

I should find that claim arrogant. Instead, only pain spreads throughout my chest. I squeeze my eyes shut and more tears trickle out.

"You could have saved them. And you could have saved me." I open my eyes and look at him. "I went through hell because they died, because I was all alone. Howie did all the things he did because I had no one."

His jaw clenches. A lump wobbles in his throat.

I get to my feet and grab the front of his shirt. "All this misery I've endured—are you saying you could have spared me from all of it?"

Xander doesn't answer. He looks away.

"Look at me!"

My fists hold the cotton prisoner. Xander looks into my eyes. I see the tears in his as well.

"Like I said, I'm not a good man, Robyn," he finally says. "I'm no hero."

"No," I agree with a shake of my head.

I look down at his shirt then let it go. Slowly, I step back.

"Robyn..."

"Don't ever talk to me again." I lift a finger in front of his face.

I turn my back to him and walk to the bed.

"Now I know why you married me, why you were so hell-bent on protecting me. And to think I was afraid I was using you." I wrap my arms around my shoulders. "You were using me."

"Robyn, I didn't know..."

"Well, I will not be your redemption," I cut him off as I shake my head. "I refuse to be."

"Maybe that's how it started," Xander admits. "Maybe we started out as two people using each other, looking for some kind of solace and redemption in each other that we couldn't find on our own. But we both know that's no longer true."

"Shut up!" I shout as I whirl around. "Enough, Xander. Enough!"

He closes his mouth.

"Now get out," I tell him in a softer but still firm voice as I point to the door.

For a moment, he hesitates. His eyes, now more green than gold, present me with a silent plea.

I shake my head. "Get out!"

Finally, Xander turns on his heel. He walks towards the door and pauses in the doorway to glance at me.

I glare with all the hatred I can muster. "I'll never forgive you."

He walks out the door, and the click as it falls shut pierces the silence of the room like a gong and my aching heart like a dagger.

I throw myself on the bed and shake as I sob. My mind goes blank as my chest wells up with pain.

I cry until the tears have run out. Then I head to the bathroom and throw up. When I'm done, I wipe my mouth and my tears. I blow my nose and stare at the bathroom mirror. Puffy eyes and a red nose stare back at me.

As my mind clears, a painful but inevitable realization dawns on me.

I can't stay here. I can't stay with the man who might as well have killed my family.

I run into the walk-in closet and grab a suitcase.

Chapter Twenty-Six

Xander

The heat on my quivering eyelids forces them open. I squint against the sunlight, then get up so that it's not on my face. I rub the sleep out of my eyes.

When I first see the treadmill, my eyebrows crease.

Then I remember.

Yesterday afternoon, Robyn found out about the part I played in her family's deaths. I left her in the bedroom with a heavy heart which I tried to ease with alcohol and cigarettes on the patio. Then I went on to the gym to sleep because the patio was too cold.

That's how I ended up here.

I get on my feet and stretch my arms and legs. I frown as I realize I've made the carpet dirty, even more so when I catch a whiff of my shirt.

Tobacco. Whiskey. And something sour.

My nose wrinkles.

I must have thrown up on the way here. Hopefully not in the pool.

I pull my shirt off and throw it aside. I sit on a bench and run my hands through my hair.

I messed up.

I knew Robyn would find out. It was inevitable. And I knew she would be angry.

What I didn't know was that her anger would cripple me so much. That look of hatred in her eyes was more than I could bear.

I rub the back of my head.

Ever since that day, I've lived in guilt. I've hated myself. I told myself I didn't deserve to be forgiven. I didn't want to be.

Until now.

I want Robyn to forgive me, to take me back. I want to take her in my arms and make love to her until everything's alright.

Love.

The word forms a knot in my chest and in my throat. I hang my head low.

Funny how that word comes up after I've just lost her.

"There he is," Geoffrey's voice breaks into my thoughts as he enters the gym. "Do you have any idea how long I've been looking for you?"

I don't answer.

"You didn't show up at breakfast and neither did Robyn."

My eyebrows arch. "She didn't?"

"So Linda got worried." He sits on the bench beside me. "I've been looking for you ever since. What? Have you been working out since dawn?"

I shake my head. "No. I fell asleep here."

His eyes grow wide. "You slept here?" He grasps my chin. "No wonder you look like shit."

"Well, I feel like shit."

"Smell like it, too. Ah, so that's what that stuff in the pool was."

I wince.

"So do you want to tell me all about it?"

I don't answer.

To my surprise, he grabs my hand. "You promised you'd tell me if something was bothering you. Don't let me watch you waste away again."

I look at him and see the concern in his eyes.

I open my mouth. "Well, I..."

"Good." Geoffrey suddenly stands up. "Since you're willing to talk, let's go back to the house, shall we? Your aunt and Jillian are waiting."

I sigh.

Oh well. It's about time I told everyone the truth.

~

"You're not the father of Robyn's baby?" Jillian reacts to my confession first.

She gets off the couch in the den, her eyes wide and her jaw hanging slack.

Linda pulls her arm and she slowly sits.

Silence falls on the room.

"I'm not," I confirm moments later. "Her ex is."

"The crazy one?" Jillian asks.

I nod.

She places her hand over her mouth.

"She was already pregnant when I married her," I inform them. "But I married her just the same because I wanted to protect her. You should have seen how she looked when she arrived at the site. It was clear she'd been through hell."

"So you saved her?" Linda asks.

I shrug. "I guess. I wanted to protect her and her baby, so I offered to marry her."

"I had a feeling you were trying to save her from something," Linda says with a sigh.

"You did?" Geoffrey throws her a puzzled look.

Linda nods. "But I didn't stop you because you seemed so intent on it."

"So you didn't love her?" Jillian asks.

"No," I answer.

She pouts.

"Not in the beginning," I add.

Jillian and Linda's eyes grow wide.

"But things changed, didn't they?" Geoffrey asks.

He seems to be the only one who's not surprised by what I just said.

"So everything works out," he continues. "What's the problem, then?"

I tell them about how Robyn's parents and her brother died and the part I played in it.

"Shit," Jillian curses.

"Language," Linda warns.

"Sorry," she mumbles. "But what are the chances?"

"I still don't see what the problem is," Geoffrey says. "So what if that same fire was the one that killed Robyn's family? It was the fire that killed them, not you."

"I could have helped put out that fire." I beat my fist against my chest. "And I could have saved more people."

Geoffrey snorts. "Maybe. Maybe not. And what guarantee is there that those people would have been her parents or her brother, hmm?"

"None," I answer. "But—"

"It's not your fault, Xander," Linda cuts me off. "You're only a man, not a god. You can't save everyone. And you know what? It's not up to you to do it."

I run my hands through my hair.

Linda sighs. "I know you like playing hero. You felt good when that man said you saved his life, and wanting to feel that way again was what helped you crawl out of the pits of hell. And you did become a hero."

She reaches for my hand and squeezes it.

"You were a firefighter and you did save a lot of lives. But you're still just human. There are things beyond your control."

"I know that." I nod. "I know that now."

"Then you just have to tell Robyn," Jillian says. "Tell her it wasn't your fault but that you're sorry all the same. Ask for her forgiveness and tell her you'll spend the rest of your life making it up to her. Tell her how you feel."

I shake my head. "She doesn't want to see me or talk to me again."

"That's because she's hurting," Linda says. "And she's pregnant, too."

"She was angry and she didn't mean it," Geoffrey says. "I'm sure of it. If you talk to her, she'll listen, and I'm sure she'll find it in her heart to forgive you."

I narrow my eyes at him. "You really like Robyn, don't you?"

"We all do," Linda answers. "We all know she's a good woman. So what if her baby isn't yours? She's your wife now, and we love her."

I look at my hands. "And if she doesn't forgive me? What if she doesn't want to be my wife anymore?"

To my surprise, Jillian punches my arm.

"What was that for?" I ask her.

"Look at you acting so cowardly. The sight of it makes me sick."

"Jillian," Linda scolds.

"You're a man, aren't you?" Jillian challenges me with narrowed eyes. "Then be a man and do whatever it takes to win her back. Don't you dare let go of her."

For a moment, I just look at her serious, scary expression. Then I grin. "I'd forgotten how much of a bully you are."

"Am not." She puts her hands on her hips.

"It's alright." I stand up and pat her on the shoulder. "You're right. I mustn't let her go. I won't."

Jillian grins. "That's more like it."

"Go talk to her," Linda urges.

I take a deep breath and leave the room. I break into a run up the second staircase.

As I reach the top, my phone beeps. I ignore it at first, but decide to check who it is.

Tyrone.

He's found something about Howie and his gang.

Good. But right now, I have more important things to deal with.

I walk briskly down the hall and stop in front of the bedroom door. I draw another deep breath before knocking.

"Robyn?"

No answer.

"Robyn, I just want to talk. You don't have to open the door. You can just listen. Just tell me you're there."

Still no answer.

"Robyn?"

When I still don't hear anything beyond the door, my shoulders sink. I walk away but stop after a few steps as a realization sinks in.

Geoffrey said she didn't show up at breakfast. What if something bad has happened to her?

In a panic, I run back to the bedroom and open the door. My eyes grow wide as they take in the empty bed. It looks as if it hasn't been slept in.

My gaze falls on the wedding band lying on the carpet.

I run to the closet and the blood drains from my face as I find her clothes and one of my suitcases missing.

No!

I punch the wall before running out of the room.

My heart races in my chest.

Where could Robyn have gone?

Chapter Twenty-Seven

Robyn

"Have a good day."

The man behind the counter hands me a small paper bag, my receipt and my change. I slip the bills inside my wallet before walking away.

Thank goodness I've got some cash. Otherwise, I wouldn't have been able to leave the house. I don't have much, though, and I'll still need to pay the hospital fees when I give birth, so I have to be careful what I spend on until then. Afterwards, I'll simply have to find a cheap daycare center and a job.

I check the contents of the paper bag, making sure my prenatal vitamins are inside. In my hurry to leave Xander's house, I forgot mine in the drawer of the bedside table. I place the paper bag inside my purse along with the receipt and walk out of the pharmacy. My eyes dart towards the sunset sky.

It's getting late. I should get something to eat and then head back to the motel.

Remembering the deli I passed earlier, I turn around and walk towards it. I walk slowly because I don't want to get short of breath, which has been happening a lot lately. A few glances go my way.

They must be wondering what I'm doing walking with a belly that looks about to burst. Alone.

My thoughts drift to Xander.

I thought I wasn't going to be alone anymore, but I guess I have no choice. I can't stay with Xander now that I know the truth.

I pause and let out a sigh.

Now that my shock and anger have faded, I know it really isn't Xander's fault. It's not like he locked my parents and Wesley inside that building and set fire to it.

I understand his guilt, though. I've spent the last few years wondering what I could have done differently— what if this and what if that—and if I might have been able to save them somehow. I've wondered countless times why I didn't die with them—and there are times I wish I had.

Maybe it's time for us to not just leave the past behind but let it go?

But I've already told him I'll never forgive him. Not that he asked for my forgiveness, exactly. Besides, what's the point of continuing with our little farce? He's already been avoiding me, probably because I'm an unpleasant reminder of his past. As he'll forever be a reminder of mine.

We'll just be reminding each other of things we'd rather forget.

Then his words come back to me.

Maybe that's how it started, but we both know it's no longer true.

What did Xander mean by that?

My thoughts freeze as I feel a chill on my nape. I turn around but don't see anyone.

Weird. I could have sworn someone was looking straight at me.

I continue walking, but I can't seem to shake off the feeling that someone's following me. Each time I turn my head, though, no one's there.

Am I just being paranoid?

Well, I haven't been alone in a while, after all. Maybe I've just gotten used to having someone by my side to protect me and now that I don't, the fear is getting ahead of me.

I shake my head and walk on a little faster.

After a few minutes, I cross the street and reach the deli.

I order one of the cheapest sandwiches they have— the grilled cheese with pastrami—and walk out with it. I continue on to the motel. This time, I don't get any more weird sensations.

See. I'm just being paranoid.

The sky has gone dark now, and the street lights are sputtering to life. I walk under them at a comfortable pace until I get to the motel. I take my key out of my purse and slip it into the doorknob. It gives a click and I turn it, then step inside.

After turning on the lights, I take off my coat and drape it over the only chair in the room. I pick up the remote control from the bed to turn the TV on.

But I never get to.

The moment I touch it, the hairs on my nape stand up again, and before I can turn my head, something clamps around my nose and mouth—a handkerchief with a strange, sweet smell.

I try to fight it as I try to wriggle free, but it's no use. The handkerchief stays around my face and my head starts to spin. My knees give way.

I hear a curse in a heavy Irish accent before I fall into someone's arms. My eyelids drop and everything goes dark.

~

I wake up to the sound of breeze rattling a windowpane. I feel the warmth of the sun on my shoulder.

Slowly, I lift my heavy eyelids. My eyelashes flutter.

My vision is a blur at first, but after a few more blinks, I find myself in a bedroom. A single bed stands against the wall and I can spot a thin layer of dust on the bare mattress. The lamp atop the set of drawers on the opposite wall has cobwebs and so does the empty bookshelf by the door. Clothes hang on the peg behind the door—a red sweater and gray yoga pants along with yellow bikini panties and...

My eyes grow wide. My stomach coils.

Those are my clothes, which means...

I glance down at my body and let out a gasp of horror. I'm sitting on a chair and I can see my bare breasts resting on my stomach, which in turn is resting on my knees. I try to stand up, but I realize my wrists are tied behind me. My ankles are tied to the legs of the chair as well.

Shit.

There's only one person who could have done this.

Howie.

I've never been in this room, though, which means this isn't the house in the woods. It must be the other one he's talking about.

The house on the lake.

He probably thinks I won't be able to escape from here.

But I sure don't mind trying. I rub my wrists together and pull them apart, but the rope is tightly fastened. I try to slip my feet out of the ropes, but the chair wobbles.

I stop. If I fall, I might hurt myself.

That didn't bother me before, but it does now, because now, it's not just me. I have a baby, and I won't do anything to put her safety at risk.

With that thought, my heart sinks and my chin drops.

I guess I can't escape after all.

Just then, I hear footsteps out in the hall. I hear voices, too.

They're coming.

I lift my chin and clench my jaw.

There's always been something that Howie's wanted to strip off me more than my clothes—my pride. Well, he won't.

He can't break me.

I may not be able to escape, but that doesn't mean all hope is lost. Someone might still come to rescue me. I have to be strong until then.

The door opens and Howie enters the door, Vaughn behind him.

I meet his gaze squarely and suppress a shudder as he flashes me his sly grin.

He sits on the mattress. "Didn't I promise you we'd meet again? And I do keep my promises."

"What do you want?" I hiss.

"Isn't it obvious?" Howie glances at Vaughn and chuckles. "You, of course. Although I must say you're not as attractive as you used to be. You've gotten... bigger."

"Right. I'm not attractive anymore, so just let me go."

"Physically you're not, but you know me." He stands up and comes closer. "I can never seem to resist you."

He takes a few strands of my hair in his fingers and brings them to his lips. My stomach churns.

"Besides, this is only temporary, isn't it?"

I hold my breath as he touches my belly. Fear creeps up my spine.

"And I do believe it will work to my advantage. After all, you can't escape with this, and..."

His hand goes up to my breast. He takes a nipple between his fingers.

I bite my lip.

"I've heard pregnant women have more sensitive bodies."

Howie leans forward and whispers in my ear.

"I'm pretty sure we'll be able to have more fun."

His hot breath makes me shudder. My muscles tense.

Howie laughs. His hand dips between my legs and I close my eyes, then open them when he lets out a curse.

"Damn it, I can't seem to reach you down there," he says with a frown. "Maybe I should just get rid of the baby, after all."

He grabs the knife tucked into his boot.

My eyes grow wide as the blade gleams in front of me. My chest tightens in fear.

"It's in the way." He presses the blade of the knife against my stomach.

"No!" I cry out.

Howie pulls the blade away. "Why not, hmm? I don't really want anything that belongs to that fucking husband of yours in my sight."

"The baby isn't Xander's," I tell him as my eyes remain on the knife.

"Liar." He brings the knife close to my skin again.

"It's yours!" I scream.

The knife clatters to the floor.

For a moment, Howie doesn't move or say a word. His wide eyes rest on my tummy. I hold my breath.

Then he laughs. Vaughn laughs as well.

My eyebrows furrow. What's so funny?

"So I knocked you up, did I?" Howie picks up the knife. "Who would have thought?"

"Not me. I would rather have any man's baby but yours."

I immediately regret the words as his eyes narrow. Again, he presses the blade to my skin.

"Don't! It's your baby!"

"So?" Howie shrugs. "I don't really want to share you with anyone."

I look at him in horror.

A monster. He's a real monster.

The blade digs into my skin.

"Please, no!" I cry out.

Tears sting my eyes.

He pulls the blade away. "What was that?"

"Please don't," I beg him as I lower my gaze.

"Well, well, well. I don't believe you've ever begged me for anything before. See, you're already breaking."

Maybe. But I don't care. I'll do anything to keep my baby alive. Anything.

Howie kneels in front of me and grips my chin. "Do you promise to do everything I ask?"

I swallow the lump in my throat and nod.

"Everything?"

"Yes," I answer softly, tears still in my eyes.

Howie laughs. "Did you hear that, Vaughn?"

"Loud and clear," Vaughn answers.

"I guess I won't be needing you anymore," Howie says. "The old Robyn is gone. I think I'll have no trouble wrapping this one around my finger. In more ways than one."

Vaughn snickers.

"Don't worry. I'll let you in on the fun later on," he promises.

Vaughn leaves and shuts the door.

I'm no longer afraid. I no longer care about what happens to me.

Howie moves behind me.

"Try anything funny or disobey me in any way and my knife will go straight into your belly," he threatens. "Do you understand?"

"Yes," I whimper.

He strokes my cheek. "Good girl."

He cuts the rope, tying my wrists with his knife. He frees my ankle as well.

"Get on the bed," he orders.

With shaking limbs, I walk to the bed and lie down on it.

"Spread your legs."

I reluctantly obey.

"And stop trembling."

That I can't seem to do.

Howie frowns, but then he shrugs. "Oh well. I'll make you tremble, anyway."

He tucks his knife back into his boot and climbs on top of me. The bed creaks.

More tears spill out of my eyes as I look up into his.

"Stop crying, will you?"

Suddenly, I hear footsteps running down the hall. The door opens.

"Boss," Vaughn says.

"What is it?" Howie asks angrily. "You know I'm busy."

"The cops are here."

Howie's eyes grow wide. My mouth gapes.

Cops?

Howie gets off the bed. I eye the knife inside his boot.

"How the hell did they get here? How do they even know about this place?"

Vaughn shrugs. "I don't know, boss."

Howie turns to me. His palm falls on my cheek.

"You told them, didn't you?"

"How could I?" I answer as I rub my cheek. "I've never been here, remember?"

"What should we do, boss?" Vaughn asks.

"Tell the men to shoot them all," Howie says.

Vaughn leaves.

Howie sits on the chair. "If you think you're going to be rescued, you're wrong. I have plenty of men here now. They're on loan from the Russians I was telling you about."

I stiffen.

"All those cops will just die and their blood will be on you."

Again, fear seizes me, but I shake it off.

I'd given up just minutes ago, but now, hope beats in my chest.

I have to fight. For my daughter. For myself.

Gunshots sound in the distance. Howie looks out the window, and I seize the chance to pull the knife from his boot and stick it into the back of his leg.

Howie lets out a yowl of pain. I run to the door.

But I can't run as fast as I used to. Howie catches me before I can get past the threshold. He pulls my hair and throws me onto the bed. Pain pierces my hip.

"You'll pay for that, bitch," Howie hisses as he takes the knife out of his leg.

He holds the bloody knife above me and my heart stops as a numbing fear spreads throughout my body.

"I warned you."

Chapter Twenty-Eight

Xander

"Drop the knife or I'll blow your brains out," I threaten Howie as I stand in the doorway.

He quickly pulls Robyn off the bed and into his arms and presses the knife to her throat.

"Shoot and she dies," he threatens in turn with a malicious grin.

My fingers tighten around steel.

Fucking asshole.

I'd love to shoot him, but I can't, not when he has Robyn.

I glance at her. "Are you alright?"

She nods, but I can see the fear in her eyes.

"She's a marvel, isn't she?" Howie chuckles. "No wonder we can't get enough of fucking her."

Anger simmers in my chest, but I try to calm myself down. I look around the room, trying to see something I can use to my advantage.

Mattress. Rope. Lamp.

"Did she tell you the baby's mine?" Howie asks.

"Yes," I answer. "I've known all along."

He frowns.

I suppress a grimace of my own as I fail to find anything useful.

"Put the gun down," Howie orders.

He holds the blade of the knife closer to Robyn's skin and she whimpers.

"Alright." I raise my hands in surrender.

"Put it down!"

I slowly go down on one knee. My eyes meet with Robyn's.

"And slide it under the bed."

I glance at his arm. She gives a slight nod.

"Do it!" Howie urges.

As my knee touches the floor, Robyn buries her elbow in Howie's chest. He drops the knife and I kick it out of his reach before pointing the gun at him.

He pushes Robyn towards me and I fall back against the wall. The gun slips from my hand and goes off as it hits the floor.

Howie leaps past me out the door. I straighten Robyn up and let her sit on the bed.

"Are you okay?" I ask her.

She nods.

I grab her clothes from the pegs and hand them to her.

She lets them fall on her lap and clutches my shoulders. "Go."

My eyebrows furrow. "But you're safe now."

"I'll never be safe if he's not behind bars," she tells me. "Go."

I know she's right. I pick up the gun and plant a kiss on her forehead.

"Wait here."

I run out of the room, down the hall and down the stairs. When I entered the house earlier, I realized that the front door was at the topmost floor; the rest of the rooms are below it, overlooking a steep cliff.

When I reach the glass wall at the top of the second staircase, Howie comes at me with a chair. The gun falls from my hand once more.

He tries to hit me with the chair a second time but I grab it and hurl it against the wall. He comes at me with a bare fist next. I dodge it and land a blow to his stomach. His next punch lands on my jaw. His leg knocks me off balance.

Okay. He does know how to handle himself in a fight. So do I, but I'm rusty.

Still, there's no way I'm going to lose.

As he tries to kick me again, I grab his leg and twist it. He falls with a yelp of pain. I aim my fist towards his face, but he rolls away.

Limping, Howie backs up against the glass wall, fists at the ready.

I wait for him to swing one and then grab it so that I can bury my elbow in his ribs. They crack. I throw him to the floor.

Mistake. That's where the gun is.

He reaches for it. I kick it against the wall, but he grabs my leg and kicks the back of my knee. I fall to my knees.

Fuck.

Howie wraps an arm around my neck. My throat hurts, but I use my strength to throw him to the floor once more.

Still, he gets up. He grabs a wooden sculpture and throws it at me. I dodge it and it shatters the glass.

I pick up one of the shards and gash his thigh. He cries out, then his jaw clenches and veins pop out on his forehead.

He runs toward me with swinging fists and I step aside. He loses his balance and falls through the broken glass, right off the edge.

He manages to catch hold of it, but it's covered with jagged glass. Blood trickles from his palms.

I stand over him and see the cliff side below him, boulders at the bottom.

He grunts with the effort of hanging on.

I think of stepping on his hands or shoving him off. Instead, I kneel down and grudgingly offer him my hand as my sense of justice prevails.

"Grab my hand," I tell him.

The sick bastard grins.

"Grab it!" I urge.

He doesn't, so I grab his hand. The other one lets go and he sinks lower.

I grimace.

"Just let me go," Howie says. "I'd rather die than go to jail."

To me, that sounds like an excellent reason to rescue him. I try to pull him up, but his bloody arm is slippery. The shards of glass on the floor cut into my skin.

"You're not helping," I tell him through gritted teeth.

Howie laughs. Then he holds his other hand up. My eyes grow wide as I see the cigarette lighter in his fingers.

"I'm going to die," he says as he puts his thumb on the spark wheel and the stone.

The flame blossoms.

"And so are you and Robyn, because if I can't have her, no one can."

He throws the lighter into an open window on the second floor.

"No!"

His arm slips and he falls. I don't stay around to see his skull get smashed on the rocks.

Instead, I run downstairs to see if he managed to set anything on fire. My heart sinks when I look inside the room. It's apparently the gang's office, housing a couple of computer desks and a lot of file folders. I'm sure the contents would be of great professional interest to the police, but Howie's lighter has spilled fuel and flame all over a pile of paperwork. Loose paper's one of the most combustible materials around, and in *my* professional opinion, the whole place is seconds away from a huge conflagration.

Shit.

I jump back just before fire fills the room. It follows me through the hallway as I head downstairs to get Robyn.

Thankfully, she's already dressed and out of the room.

"What's going on?" she asks. "I smell smoke."

"You're going to be fine," I promise her. "I'm not going to let you die."

I lead her up the stairs. She gasps as she sees the flames. They're spreading fast. The house is made of wood, after all, and quite old.

I'd better hurry.

"We'll have to go through the flames," I tell Robyn. "It's the only way."

I glimpse a curtain and pull it off its rod. I wrap it around Robyn and lift her into my arms.

"Ready?"

She nods and clings to me.

I run past the fire and up the stairs. At the top, I put Robyn down and pull the burning curtain off her. I extinguish its flames beneath my feet as I pat out the fire on my own clothes.

"Are you alright?" Robyn asks between coughs.

I nod.

Suddenly, I hear a loud creak and in the next moment the floor begins to collapse as flames pierce it from below.

"Come on."

I pick Robyn up again and rush out the door. I hear a loud crash behind us, but I keep running without a backward glance.

"Xander!" Tyrone waves at me.

I run towards him with Robyn in my arms. I see the ambulance beside him and let out a sigh of relief.

As soon as I hand Robyn to the paramedics, I sink on the grass. A paramedic kneels beside me.

"I'm okay," I tell him. "Just make sure my wife is fine."

He nods and leaves me alone.

Tyrone sits beside me. "Sure you're okay?"

I nod. "What happened to Howie's men?"

"Killed some," Tyrone answers. "The rest of them are on their way to jail."

"Good."

"Where's Howie?"

"Dead."

Tyrone's eyes narrow.

"I didn't kill him," I tell him. "He fell down the cliff side and onto the rocks."

"Ouch." Tyrone grimaces.

"And he burned the house before he fell."

"Yeah. I can see that."

I follow his gaze to the burning house.

"Fire truck is already on its way."

I nod. "Good."

"You did good." Tyrone pats my back. "You saved your wife all on your own."

I glance at Robyn, who's already strapped into a gurney.

"Then again, I had no doubt you would."

"You're the one who did the hard work," I tell him. "I wasn't wrong to think you're the best cop I know."

"And you're the best firefighter I know." He squeezes my shoulder.

I say nothing.

I hear the ambulance doors close behind me and I turn my head.

My eyes follow the ambulance as it drives away.

"Shouldn't you go after her?" Tyrone asks.

I shrug. My hand goes into my pocket and I feel the golden band I've been carrying—Robyn's wedding ring. I didn't get to give it to her, and I'm not sure if I still can or should.

Yes, I saved her life. I saved her from Howie.

But that doesn't change everything, especially not the past.

Besides, now that Howie's gone, Robyn has no reason to be with me, and I can't force her.

She doesn't need my protection anymore.

We don't have to pretend to be married anymore.

"Well?"

The ambulance disappears from sight. I exhale and slip my hand out of my pocket.

"I'll just wait for her at home."

Chapter Twenty-Nine

Robyn

I stare at the cordless phone in its cradle on the counter. It's become a habit over the past few days.

I haven't heard from Xander. Nor have I seen him since the day he saved me from Howie and from the fire. I thought he'd come to the hospital with me, but he didn't. He didn't even visit.

I haven't gone back to the house since I left, either.

I was going to keep staying at that motel, but Jillian wouldn't hear of it, so now I'm staying in her basement.

Just in the meantime. Just until after the baby is born.

"Well, has the phone talked back to you yet?" Jillian asks as she strides into the kitchen with a paper bag. "Or maybe you were trying to move it with your eyes?"

I snort.

She sets the paper bag on the counter. "Some baby stuff from the house. I thought you might need it when you give birth, which should be any day now."

I glance at my tummy. It looks bigger than ever.

"Mind you, I had to wrestle it away from Linda and Geoffrey. They want you to go back to the house."

"And Xander?" I ask.

Jillian shakes her head. "I didn't see him."

I nod.

Who knows? Maybe he's gone back to work. And why shouldn't he? There's no reason for him not to move on with his life. Now that Howie's gone, there's no need to protect me, and since he isn't the father of my baby, there's no need for him to take care of me or for us to stay married.

"I swear I'm going to punch him when I see him," Jillian says.

She sits on a stool.

"He was supposed to talk to you."

I shake my head. "He saved my life. That's more than enough."

Jillian sighs and props her head on an arm. "Are you sure? Or are you trying to convince yourself?"

I don't answer.

"Maybe I should just punch you, too."

"Maybe you should. I lied to you, after all. And I used your cousin."

"Step-cousin," Jillian corrects. "And you only lied to survive. And you didn't use Xander. He had his own motives."

"We both did," I agree. "But now those motives are gone."

"Yes, they are. So all that's left are feelings. True feelings."

"What feelings?"

She growls. "Are you honestly telling me you have no feelings for my cousin?"

"You mean your step-cousin?"

Jillian gets off her stool and grabs my shoulders. "Do you or do you not love Alexander Bolt?"

I narrow my eyes at her. "Wow. You sound like the parson at our wedding."

She lets go of my shoulders and puts her hands on her hips. "Do you love him? Don't you want to be with him?"

I don't answer.

"I know about what happened before, but does that really matter? Even if it does, it wasn't Xander's fault. You must know that."

"I do."

"Then why are you here? Why aren't you with your husband? Why haven't you picked up that phone?"

I glance at the phone. "Who said I was trying to pick it up? I was waiting for a call."

Jillian rolls her eyes. "Seriously, I want to punch both of you."

I blink.

She holds my arms. "If you were waiting for him to call, then you do have feelings for him. And trust me, he wouldn't have gone and saved you if he didn't have feelings for you, too."

I shake my head. "He probably just felt responsible."

"Really?" Her hands go up in the air then fall to her sides. "Do you really believe that?"

"I..."

I pause as I feel a stab of pain in my back. I put my hand on the spot to rub it.

"Robyn?" Jillian asks.

"I'm..."

This time, I get cut off by a tightening in my belly so intense it robs me of breath.

"Robyn, are you going into labor?" Jillian touches my arm.

Before I can answer, I feel something pop inside me. Something wet trickles down my thigh.

I look at Jillian. "I think we need to get to the hospital right now."

~

"Doctor!" Jillian shouts as soon as we enter the hospital. "I need a doctor, please! My... cousin is about to give birth."

A nurse runs towards us with a wheelchair. I sink into it and grip my stomach as it contracts again.

"Shit."

"How far along is she?" the nurse asks.

"37 weeks," I manage to answer before taking a gulp of air.

"And when did the contractions start?"

"Just about half an hour ago," Jillian answers. "But her water already broke."

The nurse inspects my leg. "Okay. Let's get you to the delivery room."

I nod and she starts to wheel me down the hall. I grab Jillian's hand with my shaking one. My heart races.

"You'll be fine," she assures me.

"Wait!"

My heart stops as I hear Xander's voice from behind me. The wheelchair stops as well.

"I called him," Jillian explains.

Xander stops beside the wheelchair, panting.

"Is he the father?" the nurse asks.

I look into Xander's eyes, and just like that, I feel suddenly calmer. Warmth swells in my chest.

"Yes, he is."

"Well, let's go, then." The nurse continues pushing the wheelchair. "This baby isn't going to wait for anyone."

Chapter Thirty

Xander

"You're doing great," I encourage Robyn as I hold her hand tight—though she's holding mine even tighter. "Just breathe and push."

She glares at me. "Easy for you to say." She huffs. "You're not the one giving birth."

"I've assisted at a few childbirths, though," I tell her. "Back when I was a firefighter."

The nurse across from me raises her eyebrow.

Robyn draws another deep breath. "Right. When you were some big hero, right?"

I frown at the remark. "Are you being sarcastic?"

"No! I'm not..." She grips my hand tighter as she pushes. "...being—Fuck!—sarcastic!"

She rests her head on the pillow and pants. "I meant it. Jillian told me all about those lives you saved. You were a real hero."

My eyebrows arch.

"You're no superhero, though," she goes on. "So you couldn't have saved my parents and my brother."

My eyebrows rise even more. "You're not mad at me anymore?"

"No." She lifts her head and starts huffing again. "It's not your fault my parents died and it's not my fault I survived."

She screams as she pushes. Beads of sweat appear on her forehead as tears break out of the corners of her eyes.

"If you're not mad at me, why didn't you come back?" I ask her.

"Why didn't you call me?" Robyn shouts as she gives another push.

"I thought you were mad at me," I answer. "And I thought you didn't need me anymore."

She lies back down. The nurse wipes the sweat off her forehead.

"And I thought you didn't need me," Robyn says as she meets my gaze.

"Could we please focus?" Dr. Strafford finally asks.

Robyn keeps her eyes on me.

"No," I tell her. "Maybe not. But…"

"Fuck!" she screams again as she sits up.

Her forehead creases from exertion. Her cheeks hollow and her face grows red.

"Push," Dr. Strafford urges. "Just a little more."

She falls on the pillow and shakes her head. "I can't do this. I can't."

"Yes, you can." I press the back of her hand to my lips. "Because you're the strongest, bravest, most amazing woman I've ever met."

Robyn's brown eyes grow wide.

"And I love you," I blurt out.

I slip the wedding ring I've been carrying with me back on her finger.

Her lips curve into a smile. "I love you, too."

Dr. Strafford sighs. "Now, can we please get on with it?"

Robyn sits up and bends forward as she grips my hand tight. Her gasps, grunts and groans spill into the air.

"Just a little more," Dr. Strafford says.

Robyn screams. A moment later, a new cry pierces the air.

Robyn lies back down with a wide, radiant smile as she gasps for breath. Her grip on me loosens but she doesn't let go.

"Congratulations." Dr. Strafford holds the baby in her arms. "It's a healthy baby girl."

The baby cries louder.

Dr. Strafford wraps the baby in Connie's rainbow blanket and hands it to Robyn. She gasps and presses the bundle to her heart, then kisses the top of her head.

As I watch her, my chest swells.

My lips curve into a smile as I look at her face, which no longer has any trace of the pain and hardship she's just gone through. Her cheeks glow on either side of the smile that seems fixed to her lips. Her eyes glisten with tears of joy.

Then my gaze goes to the baby girl and my heart stops. My breath catches.

I can't believe she's finally here.

"She has red hair like me," Robyn observes out loud as she runs a hand through the baby's fiery wisps.

"Yes, just like you," I agree.

Even if the baby had dark hair, though, it wouldn't matter. It doesn't matter who her father is, because at this moment she's a new human being. She's unlike anyone else on this earth and she's going to be whatever she wants to be. It's her life. This is her beginning, and nothing that came before matters.

"Would you like to hold her?" Robyn asks to my surprise.

I give a reluctant nod.

Robyn places the baby in my arms. As I look at her, my heart begins to pound and I feel peace and joy unlike any other. It's as if all of the scars of the past and all my fears for the future have been washed away.

"I know what to name her," I tell Robyn.

"What?" she asks.

"Renaissance," I say. "For rebirth. Because by her birth, she's also given us a second chance at life."

Robyn nods. "It makes perfect sense."

"We'll call her Raine, though," I add as I stroke her little cheek.

"Well, rain also makes things new," Robyn agrees. "It's perfect."

I think so, too. And Raine seems to agree, because she wraps her hand around my finger.

I plant a kiss on the top of her head. "Welcome to the world, Raine Bolt."

"Hey, don't forget about me." Robyn reaches for my hand.

"Never," I promise her as I squeeze her hand. "From now on, we're a family."

Chapter Thirty-One

Robyn

A family.

My own family.

The thought of it still makes my heart skip a beat, and I smile as I gaze down at Raine sleeping soundly in her crib. There's no reason for her not to now that I've just fed her and changed her diaper.

As always, I resist the temptation to squeeze her chubby cheeks or kiss her little fists.

It's only been two weeks and already she's grown. And each day, she takes up more and more space in my heart.

"Is she asleep?" Xander asks as he steps in.

I hold my finger to my lips.

He tiptoes towards the crib, then places his arm around me. I wrap my arm around his waist and rest my head on his shoulder.

"She's so beautiful, isn't she?" I whisper.

"Of course she is," Xander answers. "Because she's like her mother."

He plants a kiss on my hair.

I look at him. "Now you think I'm beautiful again."

"I never thought otherwise."

He grasps my chin and brushes his lips against mine before sealing them. I kiss him back.

"I love you." The words leave my lips as the kiss breaks.

"And I love you," he echoes as he kisses me again.

The kiss sends a flurry of heat all the way to my toes. My heart races.

I pull away. "We can't. Raine will wake up."

"Right." Xander strokes my hair. "I just wanted to kiss you."

"Yeah, right."

Xander grins, then wraps his arms around me. "You know, I was thinking..."

"Of what?" I touch his arm and lean back against him.

"Of our own house. It's about time I finish it."

I turn my head and look into his eyes.

"You mean it?"

He nods. "We should have a home of our own."

"I agree. And I do believe you have the perfect design in mind. I can't wait to see it come to life."

He presses his cheek to mine. "Neither can I."

I smile against his skin.

First, my own family. Then my own home.

My heart could burst with joy.

I look up at the evening sky through the window.

I can feel Mom, Dad and Wesley watching over me, and I know they're happy for me, too.

Finally, everything's falling into place. And all the hardships I've been through—they're fading. I don't mind them anymore.

After all, they led me to this moment, and this—this is worth all I've been through.

I glance at my husband and then gaze at the face of my daughter.

Yup. It's all worth it.

EPILOGUE

Xander

Five years later...

"Silent night, holy night..."

The music drifts above the crackle of the flames in the fireplace.

I watch them dance as I lift my glass of wine to my lips. My thoughts travel back to the fire over a decade ago.

That was a tragedy, sure, but if not for it, Robyn and I might not even have met.

"What are you thinking of?" Robyn asks as she walks back into the living room.

Her fingers wrap around her own glass of wine. The maroon couch dips as she sits beside me.

"Nothing," I tell her. "Are the kids asleep?"

She nods. "Raine and the twins are sound asleep and waiting for Santa."

I take another sip of wine. "Well, the terrible two must have been tired after running around all evening."

"Thank goodness." Robyn lets out a sigh of relief as she sits back. "Jillian said it was easier taking care of your own children, but I'm beginning to doubt it now."

"Your roles have been reversed, huh? Now she has a girl and you have two boys."

"Yup. We're even, although she's still hung up over the fact that we had twins."

I grin as I remember Jillian's reaction when we first showed her the ultrasound picture of Leo and Lucas—two in one womb. She couldn't hide her surprise, or her envy. She mellowed, though, after we promised her we'd let her throw their baby showers, which she did with twice the fanfare of Raine's.

"So..." Robyn gulps down the burgundy contents of her glass and sets it down on the coffee table. "What were you thinking of while gazing into the fire, hmm?"

I look at her. She's as relentless as ever.

"Just that we've had some great Christmases lately."

She moves closer to me. "I know. And this is going to be another wonderful Christmas."

I narrow my eyes at her. "Is it?"

Robyn nods. "Especially after you unwrap my present."

Judging from her mischievous grin, I already have an idea what it is. I wash down the lump in my throat with the rest of my wine and put down the empty glass.

"Can I do that now?"

She puts the end of the sash of her robe into my palm.

"One, two…"

At the count of three, I pull the sash and my heart pounds as I see what Robyn is wearing beneath the robe: a red lace bra trimmed with white fur that lets me see the top of her firm breasts and a matching transparent skirt. Through it, I see the bright red underwear she's wearing, and after she sheds the robe and turns around, I realize it's a thong.

My cock stiffens in approval.

"I haven't worn anything like this since our wedding night," she says as she gives another whirl in front of the tree.

The colorful lights paint her skin.

"I've just been so busy with the kids to buy lingerie, but tonight…" She climbs onto my lap and touches the tip of my nose. "Tonight, I'm going to treat us to something special."

Her hand brushes against my cock and it quivers.

I grin. "I can already tell this is the best Christmas present ever."

I wrap my lips around one of her breasts, sucking it through the lace. Robyn gasps.

"I didn't get you a present, though."

"Well, you'll just have to treat me extra special, then," Robyn says.

I narrow my gaze. "Is that a challenge?"

She just chuckles.

I flash her another grin. "Well, something extra special coming up."

I claim her mouth in a kiss as I wrap my arms around her. I slip my tongue past her lips and it mingles with hers. I taste the wine.

Robyn clutches my shoulders and kisses me back fiercely. She moans into my mouth.

I swallow her moans and savor her kisses as I run my fingers along her spine. Then I cup her bare butt cheeks and stand up.

She wraps her legs around me as she gasps.

"Where are we going?"

"You'll see," I answer simply.

I carry Robyn to the kitchen and set her down on the edge of the dining table, where I kiss her again until she's out of breath. I rub her nipples through the lace until she shivers, then pull on the bow and her breasts bounce free. I give each of them a quick, hard suck that draws a gasp.

I push her down on the table and slide her across it so that she's further away from me. Then I reach for her red thong and slide the tiny garment off her legs. I toss it aside.

"The kids better not find that," Robyn warns with a chuckle. "I wouldn't want to see Lucas wearing that on his head."

I don't answer.

I just bend over and spread her legs. I lift her lace skirt and bury my face between her thighs. I part my lips and let the tip of my tongue brush against her nub.

Robyn lets out a cry.

"Shh," I tell her. "You don't want to wake the kids, do you?"

"And let them see me like this?" She shakes her head.

She holds back her moans and cries as I continue teasing that nub, but one cry escapes when I slip my tongue inside her.

I ignore it.

I dig into my Christmas feast, tasting something better than turkey or wine.

The taste of her that I'll never tire of.

And with each swipe of my tongue, I get more and more of it. The sweet scent drifts into my nostrils.

Robyn's thighs quiver. She sits up, leaning on her elbows. Her legs bend and her feet rest against the table. Her hips rise.

I hold them down as I continue sucking and rubbing my tongue against her. I glance up to see her with her eyes squeezed shut and her lips parted. The rosy peaks of her breasts poke the air.

Continuing to tease her with my tongue, I grab one and rub it between my fingers.

Suddenly, she grips my hair. Her thighs tremble and squeeze me. Her hips jerk and her mouth gapes.

I keep licking the sweet syrup leaking out of her until she pushes my head away. She falls on top of the table and pants.

I give her no time to catch her breath.

I pull her off the table and kiss her lips. Then I turn her around and bend her over it.

I take out my cock and enter her from behind with one thrust.

She gasps.

I pound into her and her hips rock with mine. The table shakes and her gasps turn into moans. The snowman cookie jar near the other end rattles.

I pull Robyn off the table and push her down on the floor on her hands and knees. I cup her breasts as I continue pounding into her exquisite passage.

Even after three children, her velvety skin still clings to my cock and squeezes every ounce of self-control out of me.

Suddenly, I have an idea. Slowly, I stand up and lift her legs.

"Xander, what are you...?"

The rest of her words vanish as I continue pounding into her. Her nails rake the floor. Her hair tumbles down.

Heat coils in my balls and I clench my jaw. My cock quivers and leaks inside her.

Just a little more...

I pull out and drop her legs. Then I lift her back onto the table and enter her again. I slip my tongue into her gaping mouth. Her lips shudder against mine.

I grip Robyn's hips and move in and out of her, ignoring everything else. She moans louder into my mouth.

Suddenly, she clings to my arms. Her nails dig into my skin as she trembles. Her velvety core tightens around me.

I manage one more thrust before emptying myself inside her with a few jerks of my hips. Only after that do I let her lips go to chase after my breath. Her chest rises and falls as she does the same.

When I've accomplished that, I pull out and tuck myself back into my boxers and my pants. Then I lift Robyn off the table and carry her in my arms. I bring her back to the living room and set her down on the couch. She picks up her robe and slips it back on.

I reach for the bottle of wine.

"More?" I ask her.

Robyn nods.

I pour two glasses and hand one to her. Then I take a sip from mine and put my arm around her. She snuggles against me, quiet for a while as she stares into the fire.

"What are you thinking of?" I ask her.

"Nothing," she says. "Just how happy I am right now."

"Really?"

She holds my left hand and our fingers entwine. The identical golden bands gleam in the firelight.

"Thank you," she tells me.

"For what?"

"For saving me. You really are my hero."

I shake my head and plant a kiss on her forehead. "You saved me."

If not for Robyn, I'd still be wallowing in guilt. I'd still be haunted by the past. But she has set me free.

We've set each other free. And now, we can soar towards the future.

Together.

And I will protect what we have for as long as I live.

~*The End*~

Made in the USA
Lexington, KY
27 June 2018